"A

The widow's voice was as chill as the weather.

"At least—all nice men a—" She slipped, and the words ended in a shriek.

Savage grabbed for her and caught her, only to slip himself and let out a shout as they skidded down the hill.

Laughing helplessly, he sat up, the widow still clasped in his arms. "At least we came...down faster than we...went up," he gasped.

For the first time since he'd met her, she looked like a young girl. Out of breath, she said with an exaggeratedly mournful air, "But at what...cost to...our dignity!"

"Never mind about dignity—admit that whatever I lack, I make a famous toboggan."

She laughed again. "Poor soul, you took the brunt of the disaster. I hope you have taken no hurt?"

"None. For a fallen woman, Mrs. Hythe, you weigh very little and—" The merriment instantly faded from her face, though he knew not why.

Books by Gwyneth Moore

HARLEQUIN REGENCY ROMANCE
16–MEN WERE DECEIVERS EVER
27–THE DIRTY FROG

LOVE'S LADY LOST

GWYNETH MOORE

Harlequin Books

TORONTO • NEW YORK • LONDON
AMSTERDAM • PARIS • SYDNEY • HAMBURG
STOCKHOLM • ATHENS • TOKYO • MILAN

Published September 1991

ISBN 0-373-31157-5

LOVE'S LADY LOST

CHAPTER ONE

London

Winter, 1813

THE SKIES OUTSIDE were leaden and a bitter wind out of the northeast rattled the bare branches of the trees and hastened the flight of an occasional hurrying sparrow. On this chill February afternoon all the windows of the mansion on Grosvenor Place were tightly closed. The great house was quite modern, however, and had been erected by a master builder, and few draughts disturbed the heavy green velvet of the withdrawing-room draperies. If an occasional puff of smoke made a mischievous intrusion into the luxurious chamber, such a lapse was a small price to pay for the glowing logs that threw out so welcome a warmth.

One would have supposed that every occupant of the house might well have glanced out of the window and breathed a thankful sigh to be warm and snug inside. In actual fact, the withdrawing room atmosphere was scarcely less arctic than the breath of the wind that moaned across the terrace, and the two gentlemen seated by the fire looked ill at ease and anything but thankful.

The younger of the pair, a well built man, carelessly elegant in a long-tailed beige coat with gold buttons, cream pantaloons, which fit like a second skin, and a cravat that had caused his man to moan with joy, ran a slim white hand through his brown curly locks and turned a pair of heavy-lidded blue eyes on his companion. "Surely, sir," he protested with faint indignation, "you must know. I am your only son, and I'd have thought that did you not recall the day of my birth, you might at least remember the year!"

"Of course I remember it!" Mr. Boswell Savage rose from his chair and began to pace agitatedly about. "It was '83—" Alerted by his son's start, he amended hurriedly, "or '82. Some such thing. At all events, you must be near thirty years old, Leopold, and if the date of your birth occasionally slips my mind, you may be sure it doesn't slip *hers!* That's why the old lady is here, I make no doubt. And she'll blame *me,* like as not. For which I thank you!"

"My date of birth was July 1, 1784, sir," said Leopold Savage, his rather thin lips lengthening and a frown coming into the bored blue eyes. "Ergo, until July I am eight and twenty. And I fail to see why Grandmama should be in a pucker over my advanced years. Were you a touch more firm with her, perhaps—"

"Firm with her? By Gad, but I shall be firm with her! She'll not ride roughshod over me, I can tell you!" Mr. Savage squared his shoulders and nodded purposefully. He was a pleasant featured gentleman who had not allowed his eight and fifty years to impair his figure. An inch or two taller than his son, he was a credit to the most expensive genius who tailored him, and he contrived to look dashing despite the fact that his brown hair was becoming somewhat sparse.

Leopold's smile held a hint of mockery. He said, "I see no reason why she would attempt to ride roughshod over anyone, sir. After all, Gerry married last autumn, and there'll soon be a nursery for the old lady to cluck over, so—"

"How dare you imply that I would ever stoop to such vulgarity as to cluck, Leopold!"

With a great rustling of satin Lady Carlotta Hamildown swept into the room. She was frail and tiny, with snowy white hair that wound in a thick plait across the top of her head to vanish into the short curls clustered beside each ear. At seventy-five, her skin was wrinkled, her nose curved down and her chin curved up, but her blue eyes were as shrewd as they had been forty years earlier, and gave a hint of the beauty that had made her the toast of London and Paris, and won her twenty-six offers of marriage in her first Season. Her gown was of dark blue satin and lace. Her hands were covered by long white lace mittens, and in one she carried a fan, while the other rested on the back of a great fawn mastiff who plodded patiently at her side and whose head was level with her elbow.

Leopold had sprung to his feet, and both he and his father bowed respectfully.

She lifted her cheek for her son-in-law's salute, and extended her hand to Leopold. Her eyes softened as his curly head bowed over her fingers, but when he straightened she rapped her fan smartly across his wrist. "Well, rascal? Well?"

"Very well, I thank you, ma'am," he responded, deliberately misinterpreting, and drew a chair closer to the fire for her.

Lady Hamildown gave him a hard look as Boswell assisted her into the chair. "Tar!" she said.

The mastiff thumped across the room. A deep basket was strapped to his back, from which my lady proceeded to remove a bulky reticule and a bundle of lace. The reticule she set in the chair beside her. From the lace she extricated a crochet hook and an extremely tangled skein of white thread.

Well acquainted with this procedure, Leopold waited.

"You may seat yourself, Tar," decreed my lady.

The mastiff lowered himself with assorted thumps and grunts and settled his chin between his front paws.

"The word was—cluck, I believe," prompted the old lady grimly.

"And ill chosen, Grandmama," admitted Leopold, smiling down at her.

"Do you now refer to your description of my perfectly natural wish for a great-grandchild? Or to your various—er, *affaires de coeur?*"

"Really, Mama," exclaimed Boswell, shocked.

"Oh, yes," she said, choosing to receive this remark as a question, and poking the crochet hook at her tangled skein. "There was the Lady Penelope Barrington—a fishy eye, I always thought, despite that great bosom of hers; and Miss Hereward, of whom I had hopes because she is so stupid that all the gentlemen adore her; and the Honourable Nelda Rickerby who has great beauty—and a giggle that would drive me mad—but a good pair of hips for child-bearing—"

"Good God!" gasped Leopold. "But, ma'am, I—"

"And the Hammond gel—Henrietta, is it?"

Leopold stiffened. "Helena, ma'am. And if I dare remark it, I had no more than a light flirtation with any of those charming ladies."

"And considerably more than a light flirtation with half the high-flyers in London, eh?" Her keen eyes left the skein and darted up at him, taking in the proud tilt of the head, the hauteur of the dark brows, and the cynical downward twist to the mouth. "Touched a nerve, did I? Why? Because you really had a tendre for this last gel?" She saw the quickly suppressed frown, and cackled. "I thought so! If that was the case, why did you not wed her?"

"With all due respect, ma'am," he said with frigid politeness. "If I marry at all, which I have no inclination towards at present, it will be when I have found a lady worthy of becoming part of this family."

"Fiddlesticks!" cried my lady shrilly, and tossed lace, skein, and crochet hook over her shoulder, barely missing Boswell. She sprang to her feet, and before her diminutive rage Tar cowered, Boswell trembled, and her grandson stood even straighter.

"It is nigh thirty years since I carried you to your christening, Leopold Byrne Savage, and I should have carried your son to a like ceremony any time this five years! I have no wish to wait 'til I'm too old to see the boy, and so I tell you! Make your choice promptly. You may be sure I shall expect you to produce a gel suitable to join the hallowed ranks of Savages, but before you fix your mind on a princess, do not fail to remember that your great-great-grandfather was a privateer, your great-grandfather whiled away his youth carrying illicit brandy into Cornwall on dark nights, and your grandfather on your papa's side— The least said about him, the better!''

A glint of humour had banished the cynicism from Leopold's eyes during this speech, and now he threw back his head and laughed. "No, really, ma'am, you make me ashamed to offer for a lady!"

"A Savage does not know the word shame," she snapped, glaring at him. "Why do you lurk about behind my chair, Boswell?"

"I am p-picking up your lace, Mama," faltered Mr. Savage.

"And what have you to say for this son of yours, who has looks, a fine physique, a splendid pair of legs and more money than he knows what to do with, but cannot persuade a gel to carry his name?"

Scarlet, Leopold protested, "Faith, madam! I am perfectly capable—"

"Didn't ask you," she snarled. "Speak when you're spoken to. Boswell?"

"I—er, I fancy the boy has several ladies in—in mind, Mama," said Mr. Savage, avoiding his son's outraged eyes.

"They ain't no good in his mind," said my lady. "What he needs is one in his bed!" And seeing her grandson's tight lips parting, she added, "And I don't mean a lightskirt, though I could give you a list of those he's had in keeping. I fancy all London could!"

Annoyed, Leopold drawled, "You are singularly well-informed, ma'am."

"I am also very rich. My jewels will go to your sister, but I want my Portsmouth estate to pass to your son."

Leopold gasped. "But—I thought—"

"Thought I meant it for your cousin Donald, did you? Well, that is not my wish, for the boy's a blockhead. But now he's wedded that buxom Adeline Gates, and I'm getting older and want to see who will have my lord's beloved home. If you ain't married by this twelvemonth, the Portsmouth property will go to Donald, for Adeline will give him an heir, I've no doubt."

Boswell said happily, "By George, Mama! That's exceeding good of you! It is a magnificent estate."

"It is." The old lady sat down again, rather wearily. "Pity your son's too hoity-toity to agree."

Leopold frowned and said in a quiet voice, "I do not like my hand forced, ma'am."

"Do you not?" She leaned forward in the chair. "And you likely think you've more than enough properties now, eh? Then you're a fool. One never knows what's ahead." With a scornful snort she said to the mastiff, "Now will you look at the hauteur of the lad! Much will it serve him, for if he chooses to whistle a grand estate like Whitecaps down the wind for the sake of his pride—I'm done with him!" She snatched the lace that Mr. Savage offered, and brandished it at Leopold. "I can still take back the farm in Devon that I gave you, sir! Think on that!"

He looked into the fierce old face, then suddenly dropped to one knee and took up her clenched little hand. "My dear, you may take away whatever you choose—except your affection. That, I cannot do without."

"Oh, you wicked rogue!" Despite the harsh words, her fingers unclenched and went out to caress his thick hair. She said wistfully, "You are so like him, Leo. So like my dear Admiral. That's why I want Whitecaps to pass to you. If you won't obey me for your inheritance, then do it out of love for me. Will you think about it, boy?"

"Of course I will," he said tenderly.

"Good!" She bent forward, seized his face between her hands and gave him a smacking kiss. "Now be off with you. I cannot abide slush and sentimentality, and I've matters to discuss with your sire."

With a lithe movement Leopold stood, bowed, then walked to the door.

"And don't forget!" shrilled the old lady, fierce as ever. "Within the twelvemonth—or I'm done with you!"

"SHOULD OF BROUGHT the phaeton," murmured Crenshaw, folding gloved hands across his ample middle and nestling his chin deeper into the thick woollen scarf.

His employer not responding, the groom slanted a sideways glance at him. The well-cut profile was stern, the mouth thin. Crenshaw knew the signs. Mr. Leo was in one of his ugly humours. Wasn't nothing new about that. He'd had his occasional tantrums from the time he was in leading strings sure enough, and of late—since Miss Hammond up and married young Peter Cliveden—the master's bad humours had come thick and fast. Should of married the wench himself. Could of, so folks said. But when she was willing, he'd shied off. And by the time he changed his mind, she'd fallen head over tail in love with Peter Cliveden. A fine gent, Lieutenant Cliveden... "You hear anything new from Spain, Mr. Leo?" he enquired mildly.

"Only that his lordship has been hanging troopers left and right."

Shocked, Crenshaw said, "Took that corner mightly close, sir! What—ours? Whyfor?"

Savage swung the whip over the horses' heads and the curricle bounded forward. "Because they chased off after some wild pigs and wound up shooting each other, or so I heard. I fancy the mighty Wellington cannot rest without the sound of gunfire in his ears, so I'd not have thought a few pigs would weigh with him."

"He's a hard man. But a great general, they say. I reckon it'll snow afore night. What's your brother-in-law think about it, sir?"

"Mr. Cliveden rarely makes snap judgments about the weather." Savage's voice was as cold as the east wind.

"Ar. Well, he's a fine gent, that Lieutenant Cliveden," observed Crenshaw, well aware that in his present mood the military title would annoy Mr. Leo, who had yearned to get into the fighting and been straitly forbidden. "Not," he added, all innocence, "like that there Sir Conrad Furness. A nasty piece of—" He broke off abruptly as Savage turned the team off the road and halted the curricle in a shower of pebbles. "You'll have us in the ditch, sir!" protested Crenshaw, with the severity permitted a lifetime retainer.

"I'll have out of you what you're burning to say, before we go another yard," snapped Savage.

"Now then, Mr. Leo. I know you're put about because we had to leave poor Beck in Guildford, but—"

"I did not propose to be sneezed over all the way to Portsmouth, and Beck had a galloping cold."

"Not surprising," muttered Crenshaw, pulling the folds of his scarf higher.

"What's that you say? Do you imply that my valet caught the cold because of my inhumanity in obliging him to drive in an open curricle on a day when it is *not* about to snow?''

Noting the acid in the voice and the harsh line of the mouth, Crenshaw retrenched hurriedly. ''I only meant as Beck should of told you he had the cold 'fore we set out, sir. You can't be blamed.'' He thought, 'Much!' and smiled forgivingly. ''You know better'n to keep the horses standing in this wind, Mr. Leo.''

''Allow me to have some knowledge of my own cattle. And now let's have done with the round-aboutation. You've heard, I take it, of the wager I entered into at my club last evening.''

Crenshaw pursed his lips, and knowing he should be cautious, pointed out stubbornly, ''There's talk as Sir Conrad Furness is deep into Dun Territory. There's other talk, too. And Sir Everard Paynton don't like him.''

''What Sir Everard likes or dislikes is none of my affair. And, dammitall, who I choose to cry friends with is none of *your* affair!''

''Right you are, sir. And as I told Beck, it was likely a case of a glass too much brandy, and that way Sir Conrad has of a'talking people round his thumb.''

Savage's eyelids drooped. He asked gently, ''And what did Beck have to say?''

''He says as it's a deal of money. But you won the Liars' Club trophy at last year's contest, and you'll prob'ly do it again, just like you wagered. But he says as Mr. Boswell was mad as fire, and—''

"The devil!" That harsh utterance made Crenshaw jump and set the horses to fidgeting nervously.

Savage dropped his hands, then sent the whip snaking out again, and the curricle lurched onto the road. In a rasp of a voice, he said, "If ever I heard such insolence. You may have been in our service forever, Crenshaw, but that don't give you the right to gossip about me in the servants' hall! For two pins, I'd turn you off!"

Alarmed by their speed but not by the threat, the groom said, "If you keep on at this pace, Mr. Leo, you'll turn us *over!* Slow down, do!"

For answer, Savage whipped the team to an even more reckless pace. Above the bluster of the wind and the thunder of hooves, he shouted, "If I choose to wager two thousand guineas with Furness, or ten thousand guineas with the—the Archbishop of Canterbury, it is *my* affair and no one else's!"

"Yessir. But I don't like the sound of our back wheel. I told you so arter we left Guildford, and if you'd of listened 'stead of looking so black as any tar barrel—''

"And I am of no mind to endure your carping and nagging all the way to Portsmouth!" overrode Savage wrathfully. "You may hire yourself a room and buy a ticket on tomorrow's London stage."

Dismayed, Crenshaw pleaded, "Come along now, Mr. Leo. Don't fall into one of your starts again. You know it's not me you're vexed with but—" He grabbed the side of the rocking vehicle and gasped, "Gawd!" as the curricle raced into the yard of a small inn and came to a plunging halt.

"Out!" snapped Savage, tearing some flimsies from his purse and thrusting them at Crenshaw.

The faithful groom snatched up his valise. "Now—now, Mr. Leo..." he wailed, but the curricle was gone before he could close his mouth.

Half an hour later, with a disgusted look at the darkening grey of the skies and the occasional snowflakes that drifted down, Savage bitterly cursed the treachery of England's weather.

Crenshaw had been right, as usual. It was, he thought, all of a piece. It had been a disastrous week from start to finish. First Grandmama, trying to bully him to the altar; then that revolting fiasco at the tables; and this morning, the confrontation with his father. He should have had more sense than to go into Watier's last night. Indeed, he'd not have done so, if Ev Paynton hadn't been so insistent. Drunk, but insistent. He had almost gone home when Conrad Furness had driven the stakes so damned high, but Furness had laughed at him, and to have left at that point might have been construed a retreat. Everyone knew that Furness had pretty near ruined himself with his gaming, and that he'd been trying to recoup when he'd backed himself so heavily to win the Liars' Club Championship Match last Spring. He had lost with good grace and held no grudge against the victor, but Savage had since felt obliged to accommodate the baronet whenever he was asked to join a game. As luck would have it, he had invariably risen the winner, which had begun to be embarrassing, but Furness only said jovially that he would even the odds by snabbling the prized Trophy at the Liars' Club Match this year.

Savage scowled at the horses' ears. Furness was his senior by six years and had always been a good fellow. Handsome, in a dark and florid way, well born, polished and urbane, he was much admired but never too haughty to befriend a younger man. A fine sportsman, he was often to be found at the races or some sporting event, but it was true that lately there had been whispers of less than sportsmanlike behaviour. Not one to either lightly condemn or to easily make friends, Savage thoroughly detested rumour mongers, and saw no reason to turn his back on a man with whom he'd been acquainted for most of his life.

Last night, Furness had poured the Madeira with a liberal hand. Sir Everard Paynton had got himself into a pickle at the table, and somehow, while Savage strove to extricate his friend, the wine must have gone to his head. He really couldn't recall all of it, but he had eventually agreed to a small wager, and in a most odd fashion as the night wore on, he had yielded to Furness's urging to a bet of larger import, and had woken up this morning horrified by the realization that he had wagered two thousand guineas he would win the Cup again this year.

The gabble-mongers had been busy. At eleven o'clock he'd been summoned to his father's study. An even tempered gentleman, Papa, and seldom one to fly up into the boughs. He'd flown into them today. With a vengeance. Was Leopold aware, he'd snarled, that Grandmama Hamildown was at daggers drawn with Lady Jemima Furness, Sir Conrad's grandmother? Had he forgot his own promise to Grandmama to quit The Liars' Club? Did he know that Grandmama had told Lady Jemima that he would have no more contact with so immoral an organization? Now the fat would be in the fire indeed! Lady Hamildown was already irked because he had not married Helena Hammond (whom she had not discovered until Miss Hammond was Mrs. Cliveden). Was he absolutely yearning to be stripped of the Devonshire farm, as well as that magnificent estate in Portsmouth?

His head had been pounding brutally, and he'd been angry with himself, which had not helped matters. He had engaged in a rare and furious quarrel with his father, who had suddenly—as he could upon occasion—become the icy grand seigneur. As a result, Leopold had been ordered to at once leave the metropolis and go down to Portsmouth to face Grandmama in person.

One did not disobey one's sire, even if one set out burning with resentment of such cavalier treatment. His temper had worsened when Beck snuffled and sneezed all the way to Guildford. Plagued by the guilty knowledge that he should not have taken the curricle and exposed his servants to the bitter weather, his headache also had worsened. Now, having rid himself of both his loyal retainers, he told himself that he was glad to be alone. He was also cold and hungry, and when a snug little hedge tavern came in sight near Chawton, he turned off the Portsmouth turnpike and into the yard, and gave his team to the care of the blanket-wrapped ostler.

The simple fare was hot and satisfying, the ale was excellent, the dining room had a roaring fire, and the host, a former rifleman, had some fascinating anecdotes of the retreat from Corunna that held Savage spellbound for over an hour. It was past four o'clock when he left, and the afternoon drawing in. Accompanying him to the curricle, the host shivered when he saw the snow, and gave it as his opinion they'd have a heavy fall before morning. Savage was tempted to stay the night, but it was a straight run to Portsmouth, and not looking forward to another unpleasant interview, he was eager to get it over and done with. The team was rested, and he drove out of the yard flourishing his whip at the host and followed by a shouted admonition to come back if the road was too icy. He had no intention of coming back. His own suite awaited him at Whitecaps. The great house was always delightful, the staff eager to please. There would probably be some lively company, and when he had coaxed Grandmama out of her pet, he would enjoy some of her excellent port.

His temper improved. The improvement lasted until some twenty minutes later when a constable swathed in a greatcoat and shawl waved him to a halt. A big oak had come down across the road a mile ahead; the turnpike was impassable, and he must detour at the crossroad. It was a fair enough lane, and would take him west for a mile or so, but at the next crossroad, which was just past Davidson's barn, he could swing east again, and pick up the turnpike road beyond the hamlet of More-or-Less.

Savage looked at him suspiciously.

"No, that be the name, zur," confirmed the constable, grinning even as he stamped his feet up and down to keep warm. "More-or-Less. Only it be summat less than more, to say truth. Best not waste time, zur. Be dark soon, and whatever hasn't froze already will freeze then, sure-ly."

Savage thanked him, and sent his horses on to the crossroad. The lane was quite respectable, as the man had said, but he seemed to drive a great while before coming to a barn, and after that there was no sign of

a second crossroad, nor any signpost indicating
More-or-Less. The snowflakes were larger now, and
with the failing light, sure enough, came a dropping
of the temperature. His breath formed small clouds
in the frigid air, and he cursed himself for a fool not
to have brought the phaeton. Shivering, he drove on
cautiously, fearing the horses' hooves might slip on
the increasingly treacherous surface.

At last his keen eyes detected the second crossroad, but the lane had twisted and turned so that he
could no longer be sure which way was east. He took
what he hoped was the correct fork, but had gone
only a short distance before he pulled up, and stared
in astonishment. It had been a long time since he'd
seen any sign of human habitation, but beside the
road a very small damsel, wearing a knitted bonnet
and with a long cape over her woollen gown, held out
her skirts and danced around a puddle.

He had little experience with children, and not the
slightest wish to increase his knowledge, but that she
should not be out alone at dusk on such a cold day
was too obvious to be ignored. He said guardedly,
"Good afternoon."

The thin piping wail that had accompanied her
dance ceased, and she spun about, jumped up and
down twice, then ran to the curricle and reached up
her arms. "Him comed," she said, beaming at him.

He was forced to own that she was enchantingly
pretty, with golden curls peeping round the edges of

her bonnet, and huge blue eyes that sparkled trustingly. But she must not be more than five or six years
old at the outside. He asked, "Where are your people? Er—your papa—mama?"

For answer she pointed first to the sky and then off
to the right. "Up," she demanded, waving her arms
imperiously.

"My child," he advised her quellingly, "I have no
desire to take you up with me."

Unquelled, she laughed and repeated, "Up!"

He swore under his breath, but it would soon be
dark, and so with great reluctance he climbed down
and lifted her to the seat. Swinging up beside her, he
pulled a rug over her knees, and took up the reins.
"Is your village nearby?"

She nodded.

"Can you direct me, Miss...?"

She beamed at him, nodded again, and pointed to
the right.

Savage drove ahead a little way, looking for the
turning, but an insistent hand tugged at his sleeve,
and the child once more pointed to the right.

"So you said," he agreed dryly. "But there's no
road."

She nodded with vehemence, and he pulled up
hurriedly as she began to clamber down.

"Great heavens! Have a care!" he snapped.

Nimbly, she ran back a little way, then motioned
to him.

Savage hesitated, then contrived to turn the team. Sure enough, rutted tracks led off into the woods. The landlord, he thought, had confirmed that the hamlet was called More-or-Less, perhaps it was too much to have expected a proper lane. He guided the team into the tracks. The child was dancing again. 'Probably too half-witted to know it is nigh to freezing,' he thought. He reached down, she reached up, and in a twinkling she was seated beside him.

She was quiet for a while, but when they entered the trees, she began to sing, her piping voice achieving no recognizable melody.

"You had better tell me your name," he suggested.

The song ceased. She said with a great exhalation of breath, "Consul," smiled sunnily at him, then launched into her melody again.

"It is da—dashed near freezing," he advised the horses' ears. "The Lord only knows where we are. The off back wheel sounds ominous. And to add insult to injury, this repulsive child must sing. I wish someone could tell me why."

Consul looked up at him, obviously attempting to understand his monologue. There came again the deeply indrawn breath. She said, "Her always sings. Speshly when her's feared."

"At least," he remarked, "you've sufficient between your ears to be afraid. If ever I heard of such a thing! A mite of your years frippering about the countryside alone at dusk! You would be fair game for some gypsy, and had I not come along, my lass, you might well have wound up in a flash house. As I shall tell your parents, do we ever unearth the sorry clods. I wonder you're not blas—downright snivelling with fright!''

The blue eyes searched his features solemnly, then that great beaming smile illumined her face, and she reached up and patted his cheek. ''Her finded their knight a'armour,'' she pointed out, as if that was all that need be said of the matter.

Savage jerked his head back. ''Never try to turn me up sweet, you miniature conniver. I'm inured against feminine wiles, and so I warn you.''

She looked puzzled, and for a minute or two was quiet, but it was hushed and dim amongst the trees, and soon she was cuddling closer against him. She tugged at his sleeve, and when he bent to her, the little hand covered her mouth and she looked around as though concealing a vital secret from scores of lurking spies. ''Dark,'' she whispered.

''Let that be a lesson to you,'' he said sternly.

She shot up on the seat and let out a screeching, ''*Boo!*''

The horses neighed and plunged in terror. Savage battled to prevent a runaway, and Consul squealed with laughter. ''Deuce...take it!'' he raged, when he had at last quieted the alarmed animals. ''Do not *ever* make such a foul outcry! Had the team bolted through these trees we'd both likely be dead!"

She sobered and gazed up at him, her great eyes very round. Then, she patted his knee and said blithely, "Don't worry. Her take care 'a him."

"Good God!" muttered Savage.

"Yes," she agreed, and the song went on.

He was pondering her background when they came out of the trees. The hamlet spread directly ahead. Nestled on the slope of a hill, it presented a charming picture, with smoke winding up from the chimneys, and snowflakes beginning to whiten the thatched roofs of the dozen or so cottages. The track became a fairly decent lane now, and Savage followed it, searching for a smithy or an inn.

There were not many people about on such a frigid day, but those that were in evidence stopped and stared, and two young boys followed. Almost, thought Savage, as if the village had been isolated through a century or so, and they'd never before seen a gentleman's curricle.

"Which is your house?" he asked.

Consul sang on.

"You do live here?"

She stopped singing and smiled at him, then shook her head.

"Oh, Egad!" he groaned.

She prepared her lungs. "Wheel's broke," she offered in her explosive fashion.

He had good reason to believe her and was grateful to perceive, at the far end of the street, a tiny inn. He pulled up in front, climbed out of the curricle and looped the reins through the ring on a post, then turned back to lift Consul down.

"Arternoon, zur."

The host had come out of the inn and stood clutching a greatcoat about him and nodding amiably.

"Good afternoon," returned Savage, starting for the door with the child in one arm.

The host stood immovably on the threshold.

Irked, Savage said, "Stand aside, please. You'll not object do I come in?"

"Full up, zur."

Savage stared at him. "A brisk trade, is it? Surprising, considering I'd never have found the place had it not been for this little girl."

"Ar. You got a bad wheel there, I do see."

"Yes. And I would like to order tea and cakes while it is repaired. Be so good as to—"

"Cannot be repaired in Dingly Down, zur."

"*Dingly-Down?* The devil you say! I thought this was More-or-Less!"

"More or less Dingly Down," said the host, then roared with laughter at his witticism, his mirth echoed by the small crowd which was gathering.

Not in the least amused, Savage demanded, "Then where the hell is More-or-Less?"

"Ar, well," said the host, wiping his eyes. "That do be five miles nor'east, give or take a mile. I doubt as ye'd get there. Not with that there wheel. Splitting, it be."

"I am aware." Again attempting to get into the front door, Savage was met by bovine immovability. "What the *devil*—" he roared, then stopped. Consul was stroking his cheek and looking at him anxiously. Restraining himself with an effort, he snarled, "Were it not for the child, fellow, I'd Dingly Down you! Now—where is your smith?"

"Lun'on, zur."

"*What?*"

The host waited through the laughter that greeted this incensed reaction, then said with a broad grin, "Ar. Left 'smornin'. Won't be back 'til ... oh, three week last Friday, I reckon."

Seething, Savage gritted through his teeth, "Then where can I get a room for the night?"

The host looked dubious. "With her?"

"Lord bless us—no. I'll have to take her home first. Do you know where she lives?"

"Ar. And likely they can put you up fer the night, zur. Ye'd best go there."

"You are all consideration," said Savage ironically. "And where—pray tell—is there?"

"Why—The Widder's, a'course." The host looked at him as if he were ripe for Bedlam and there were murmurs of incredulity from the spectators. "Go back to the lane, turn right and keep on three more mile. A big white house just past the gates. Can't miss it.''

"Thank you," grunted Savage, "for your inestimable hospitality."

"You're more than welcome, zur. And you shouldn't be wandering about, missy, and well you knows it."

Consul beamed and reached out to him. The host fairly leapt back, and in a twinkling was inside, the door slamming behind him.

Lifting the child back into the curricle and ignoring the grinning onlookers, Savage muttered between his teeth, "Dingly Down—haven for the demented! Lord, what a week! At least it cannot get any worse!"

An hour later, riding one of the horses, leading the other, and with Consul snuggled up in front of him, he knew he had been overly optimistic. The wheel had split about a mile after they'd reached the lane. Cursing himself for having chased Crenshaw away, he had unharnessed the horses, strapped his valises to one of them, abandoned the curricle and started off. The only rug he carried was wrapped about the child. He was freezing cold, his head still ached miserably and every time he thought of Dingly Down his rage mounted.

"Her home," murmured a small voice.

Savage glanced down. From her cozy nest the child smiled at him.

"Will your papa be there?" he asked.

She shook her head. "Milor' an' Mama, an' Brettoe, an' Netty."

'Milor'...' "Hmm," he grunted, turning through some heavily imposing gates into the drivepath and riding towards the large two-storey house that loomed up through the dark. "Does your mama look like you?" he asked in an afterthought.

Consul gathered her breath. "Oh, no, Mama's *boo*tiful!"

Savage brightened. The host in that miserable hamlet had said The Widder's. 'Milor' was likely the child's grandfather. A beautiful widow could compensate for a certain amount of all this misery—for a time, at least.

He set Consul down in front of the house and dismounted wearily. The little girl danced up the steps and pounded at the door.

Savage tied the reins to a tree, and followed her. He heard footsteps inside, then saw the gleam of a lamp. 'The Widow cometh,' he thought, and arranged his mouth into his most appealing smile.

The door swung open. The lamp, high-held, shone brightly onto the young woman who stood there.

Savage's smile died away.

She was of average height and shapely enough. But her untidy brown hair was threaded with grey, her pale green gown was creased and her face was covered with spots.

Before he could speak, she screamed faintly, dropped to her knees and, setting the lamp aside, gathered the child into her arms. "Oh, thank God! Thank God!" she sobbed, her eyes closed. Looking up then and blinking away tears, she said brokenly, "How we have...worried! Where *ever* have you been?"

The little girl patted her cheek and beamed up at Savage. "Him taked her to Dingdong."

"What?" The woman sprang up and fixed Savage with a fierce glare.

He lifted one gauntletted hand and drawled with icy disdain, "Allow me to point out that it was my belief she lived there."

Exasperated, the woman shook the child. "How many times have I told you to stay in the garden? You are *very* naughty to have caused—"

The little girl tugged at her skirts. Her face aglow, she announced, "Mama! Her *finded* our knight a'armour! Jus' like you—"

"Hush!" The spotty face flushed, which, combined with reddened eyes and straggly hair, did nothing to improve the woman's appearance. Standing, she glanced at Savage and said with obvious reluctance, "I suppose you had better come in, but—"

"I find myself so overwhelmed by your gratitude," he began haughtily, "that I . . . must refuse your hos—hos—" He sneezed.

The woman gave an impatient exclamation. "Oh, for goodness' sake! It's freezing. Come in, do!"

"Him come!" cried Consul, seizing Savage by the leg. "Him come!"

Attempting a refusal, he was staggered by child plus sneeze. The wind sent snowflakes and his hat whirling into the hall, Consul tugged harder, and willy-nilly, he was inside and the door closed behind him.

CHAPTER TWO

IN VIEW OF the unprepossessing appearance of his hostess, Savage was surprised to find himself in a gracious and immaculately kept home. The warm air held the mingled aromas of burning logs, cooking and beeswax. A tastefully arranged bowl of holly and branches of catkins brightened a fine old mahogany sideboard in the entrance hall, and a costly rug was spread on the mellow gleam of the pegged oak floor.

From somewhere above, a hoarse voice croaked an enquiry as to whether ''Missy'' was home.

''Her home!'' howled Consul. ''Mama—her go Netty?''

''Yes, yes. Take off your cloak and change those wet shoes at once. I'll come up and wash you in a minute or two.''

The child started away, then returned to drop a wobbly curtsey which wobbled into a necessity to clutch Savage by the leg once more. She patted his knee, beamed up at him, then scuttled to the stairs. Watching her, he thought glumly that she did not at all resemble her mama. He stalked over to retrieve his hat and remove the dint from the high crown. When he looked up, the woman was watching him speculatively.

She said, "I think I must indeed thank you. And my name is Mrs. Hythe, sir."

He bowed. "I am Leopold Savage." Unsmilingly, he turned to the door. "Good day to you."

"One moment." Her hand went up in a gesture he thought ridiculously autocratic. "Did you touch Consuela?" she demanded.

A corner of his mind registered the fact that the child was Consuela, not Consul. The rest of his mind was fairly dizzied with wrath. "*Touch* her, madam?" he snarled. "'Pon my soul, but if you dare to imply—"

"Because if you did," she interrupted, "I can only hope you've had it. I doubt I am still contagious, but I've had both my cousin and my housekeeper laid down upon their beds, and although I will acknowledge the responsibility, I simply cannot undertake the care of another invalid."

"Oh," he said, the wind taken out of his sails. "Er, had—what, ma'am?"

She pushed back a lock of her tumbled hair rather wearily. "Chicken pox."

He had feared smallpox, and gave a sigh of relief as he informed her that he had suffered the affliction at the age of seven.

"It's bad enough, then," she sighed, leading the way into the darkened withdrawing room.

"And much worse when one is an adult, so I'm told." Savage took up a taper and proceeded to light a branch of candles from the widow's lamp. "I presume you are a victim, ma'am?"

The brightness of the candelabra revealed a withdrawing room not luxurious, but that was charming and comfortable and contained some beautiful pieces of furniture. The tall case clock in one corner was undoubtedly antique and of considerable value, and he would have been proud to own several of the fine paintings and sketches that hung on the walls.

Mrs. Hythe had not responded, and he glanced up to again find her watching him in that odd, intent way.

Her eyes fell at once. She said, "Yes. Though I'm better now. Almost."

Still holding the taper, he scanned her. She did not look better. He realized belatedly that the dark smudges under her eyes, the look of exhaustion, were from illness, and the grey streaks in her hair were not the result of years. He frowned, and with a guilty feeling of having judged unkindly said, "I think you should not be doing heavy housework, Mrs. Hythe."

"What makes you think I have been doing so, sir?"

"You must have been sitting still for a very long time to have cobwebs form in your hair."

Her hand flew up. She combed out a grey tendril and recoiled with a horrified, "Ugh!"

He laughed, then frowned again as a gust of wind rattled the front door. "Jove! My horses! I must go."

She hurried across the hall with him. "It is a dreadful night. Have you far to go, Mr. Savage?"

He hesitated. "To say truth, I had hoped to put up in Dilly Dally, or whatever the deuce it's called, but I appeared to be decidedly *persona non grata* in the area."

"Dingly Down. And I fear it was Consuela who was unwelcome, not you, sir."

"Indeed? She may be a scamp, but I'd have thought—"

"She is *not* a scamp!" The widow fixed him with a hostile glare. "Everyone in Dingly Down loves her. Only—she chances to live in a house full of chicken pox."

"Ah, yes, of course. I suppose she was the first victim?"

She nodded. "Fortunately, she had a very mild case. Did someone in the village send you here, Mr. Savage?"

"The tavern keeper. He said 'The Widows,' and I thought..." He paused. Her unkempt appearance was now explained, and she was certainly a lady of breeding.

"And you thought Mr. Turnbull referred to a boarding house. There is no need for you to keep your tongue between your teeth, sir, because that is exactly what we are. Of a sort. Mama and I take in paying guests at times. Usually in the summer, when it is very pretty hereabouts. Artists and people from Town come to see the old abbey, or to paint it, and the inn only has three guest rooms."

"But I cannot suppose you take in paying guests when you have a bevy of sick people to care for." He opened the door and was staggered by an arctic blast garnished with snowflakes.

"Good gracious," gasped Mrs. Hythe, pushing the door shut. "You certainly cannot travel tonight. You may have our best guest room, and I shall charge you a very high rate for what will likely be extremely poor service, so pray do not feel you impose. Give me a moment to get my cloak and I will show you where to stable your horses."

"You will do no such thing, ma'am. Only tell me where to—"

He was interrupted as the door swung open again, and a tall thin young man came in, the capes of his coat flying, and snowflakes clinging to his tousled fair hair. He peered at Mrs. Hythe with a pair of singularly fine grey eyes that held a look of great anxiety.

"Cannot find a trace of the imp," he gasped breathlessly as he slammed the door against the wind. "Has she—"

"This gentleman brought her home, thank heaven," interrupted Mrs. Hythe. "She is quite all right, dear. Mr. Savage, this is my cousin, Mr. Barrett Elstow.''

"Oh, jolly good," exclaimed Elstow, extending a gloveless hand. ''Is that your curricle along the road, sir?''

''Yes.'' Savage endured an icy grip. ''A split wheel, unfortunately. Mrs. Hythe has been so kind as to offer me accommodation for the night. Now, if you will excuse me, I must see to my horses.''

"I'll give you a hand. Er—you're not related to Mr. *Leopold* Savage, by any chance?''

''Very much so,'' said Savage with a grin. ''Why? Never say my infamous reputation has preceded me?''

Elstow stared at him for an instant, his eyes expressionless. ''Not infamous, certainly. But I did hear you'd entered into a sizable wager with Sir Conrad Furness.''

Savage heard a muffled exclamation behind him and turned to find Mrs. Hythe watching him with a shocked expression. The lady disapproved of gambling, evidently.

''Very true,'' he drawled. ''I frequently enter into wagers. It is among the least deplorable of my habits. The news has travelled fast, for we only made the wager last night.''

Elstow reached for the door handle. ''I enquired for Consuela in More-or-Less, and two gentlemen at the inn were discussing it with a good deal of animation."

"And a good deal of wine, no doubt," said Savage with a smile.

Mrs. Hythe said stiffly, "Barry, you should not have gone out without a hat. You are just up from a sickbed."

"Wind took it, dash it all." He gave a wry shrug. "It was my new beaver, too!" He peered rather myopically at his cousin. "Good God, Prim, if you don't look a proper fright! What's all that horrid stuff in your hair?"

Embarrassed, she said, "Cobwebs. I went down into the cellar, searching for Consuela."

"Egad! I wonder Mr. Savage didn't run off screaming. In all fairness, sir, I must tell you my cousin Primrose don't always look quite so—"

"Thank you, Barrett," interrupted Mrs. Hythe, scarlet. "You'd best hasten. As soon as I get Consuela into bed, I shall serve dinner. Did the wind take your gloves also, dear?"

He gave her a guilty look. "Forgot 'em. Come along, sir. We'll tend to your cattle, and I'll help you carry up your gear. Those are valises I saw tied to your hack, no?"

Savage verified this and the two men went outside. The wind had grown colder and much stronger and sent their coats flapping, while great flakes of snow drove at their faces. Luckily, Savage had teth-

ered the horses under a tree, which had protected
them to an extent, but he was glad to get them into
the spacious barn, and more than glad to have Elstow's assistance in unharnessing, rubbing down and
feeding them.

The young man, who appeared to be of an amiable disposition, asked no questions, but said it
would be "jolly good" to have another male to talk
to.

"Not that Primrose—my cousin Hythe, is a widgeon," he went on rather apologetically. "Indeed,
she can converse knowledgeably on many subjects.
But—poor little soul, she's been quite ill, and with all
the responsibilities on her shoulders has no time to
sit and chat."

"Has she just the housekeeper to help her?" asked
Savage, busied with oats and nosebags.

"She hires another maid in the summertime. And
my Aunt Ethel, Prim's mama, you know, spends the
winters with her sister in Cornwall, but she is here
during the warmer months. She is frail and—not to
in any way criticize the poor lady—is inclined to be
more of a burden than a help. I do most of the work
with the animals and try to keep the grounds up. But
I'll own to being a not vastly efficient workman."

Since he had at first helped willingly enough, but
then stood watching as Savage worked, this statement was believable.

"Be a good fellow and feed the mare, will you?" asked Savage easily. "I'm going to give this lad a rub-down."

Elstow complied without resentment, exclaiming over the mare's points and contriving to spill as many oats as entered the nosebag.

"Do you live here permanently?" asked Savage, adding with his twisted grin, "By all means tell me to keep my nose in my pocket, if I impose."

"Not at all, sir. I came down from Oxford two years back. I'd intended to stay and try for a Fellowship, but Prim had to turn off her groom and the butler, and I don't like her to be alone here. She's a widow, you see." He stood staring into the nosebag, which he held just out of reach of the frustrated mare. "Not safe," he muttered.

Savage darted a keen glance at him. "I'd have judged you no more than one and twenty. You must have taken your Tutor by storm. Which is your college?"

Elstow smiled at him in a vague way, then staggered as the mare made a determined lunge for her dinner. "My apologies, ma'am," he said, fastening the bag over her head. "I think we shall have to throw blankets over 'em, don't you sir? Going to be beastly cold tonight." He picked up some straw and started to help Savage. "I am twenty-two, actually. My Tutor was an awfully good old boy. Merton."

"Indeed? Are you to become a man of the cloth, then? Or—your pardon, perhaps you already are in Orders?"

"No, no, sir. I was intended for the clergy, of course. But I developed a frightfully deep interest in architecture. That's one of the reasons I'm here, d'you see?" It being clear from the lift of one of Savage's brows that he did not see, Elstow elaborated. "The old place. You saw it when you rode in, I fancy."

"It was too dark to see much of anything." Savage took the handful of straw from Elstow's lax grasp. "I'll finish here. D'you suppose you could find those blankets?"

Elstow ambled off, his voice taking on an echoing quality as he rummaged about. "It's quite famous, you know. That's why so many artists come in the summer. William of Normandy bestowed the original grant upon one of his retinue, who built a castle here. The cellars are the only part of that structure remaining. The abbey was built a couple of centuries later."

Savage gave a start and stared into the shadows where Elstow had disappeared. Small wonder this barn was so vast. "Do you say that Erskine Abbey is *here?* On this property?"

"Yes, sir. This was the steward's house. The abbey is atop the hill. Not much left of it nowadays. But it's a lovely old place. Or was, that is." He laughed merrily. "Now there's a scrambled sentence for you! I wrote a pamphlet on it. The abbey, not the sentence. Quite a success, if I dare say so. At the moment, I'm working on a study of the influence of nationalism on British architecture... Most fascinating."

The last few words were difficult to distinguish. His voice droned on, fading eventually into silence. Savage, not noted for patience, began to be irked. His call brought no response, and he took up the lamp Elstow had lighted and went in search of the young man.

Far at the end of a long line of stalls, only four of which were occupied, Elstow sat on a bale of hay clutching two blankets. He smiled dreamily as Savage came up. "Really tragic," he murmured, "when these Germans and Italians are brought in and take a perfectly delightful design and fripper it up with— Oh, I say!" He sprang to his feet, his fair skin reddening. "I do apologize. You've been waiting. Afraid I'm an awful wool-gatherer, sir."

"Do you know, I'm inclined to believe you." Savage took charge of the blankets. "So Mrs. Hythe has fallen heir to the ruins, has she? Is the place not entailed?"

"Yes. But the provisions are rather—"

"Really, Barry," said an indignant feminine voice. "I am very sure Mr. Savage has no least interest in our family matters!"

A warm woollen pelisse wrapped about her, Mrs. Hythe stood watching them and looking vexed.

Elstow's fading flush flared into a blaze once more. "No, but—er, really Prim, I wasn't exactly—"

"I fear I am to blame for keeping Mr. Elstow talking, ma'am," said Savage blandly. "I gather I have stumbled upon a much admired antiquity."

In return for his friendly smile he received a faintly contemptuous stare. "My father taught me always to beware of a gentleman with a silver tongue," she observed. "Dinner is getting cold."

He was unaccustomed to being snubbed, and he experienced a burning desire to give Mrs. Prim the set-down she warranted. Since she was an ailing lady, he restrained himself, however, and kept grimly silent as they returned to the house.

Equally silent, Elstow conducted Savage upstairs to a large and well-appointed room, dominated by a great mahogany four-poster. He tossed the valise and carpet-bag onto a bench at the foot of the bed. "Pray do not be offended by Prim's rather—er, abrupt way, sir. She has been ill and—and has much to bear."

Savage sat on the bed, and only then realized how tired he was. "Well, I'll remove one of her cares when I leave in the morning. Gad, but this is a fine feather bed!"

"Yes. Old Turnbull tried to buy it when my Uncle John went to his reward, but Prim—" He stopped abruptly. "How my tongue does rattle on."

"I'll not betray you. Er, Consuela mentioned a Milor'..."

"Yes. She's likely with him now. She pretends to read to him, dear little thing. Not that he understands a word she says."

Savage asked uneasily. "Shall I see him at dinner?"

"Good Lord—no, sir! My cousin don't allow him in the dining room. Especially when we've guests in the house. His behaviour's a trifle—er, unpredictable."

So insanity ran in this extreme odd family! 'Likely has to be kept locked up,' thought Savage, and decided that the sooner he departed, the better.

He washed in the hot water Elstow brought him, brushed his thick hair and put off his riding dress. Confident that his snowy cravat was well tied, that his grey coat was a triumph of tailoring and that his jewelled quizzing glass could be wielded with devastating effect if the widow cut up rough, he strolled into the hall.

Consuela scampered up the stairs, wearing a much patched dressing gown. With a conspiratorial beam, she put a finger to her lips. "Her begetted to say 'night to Milor'," she whispered as she passed him.

"I see," he said, whispering also. "Where is he?"

"In a' drawing room."

"Thank you." He started down the stairs.

Over her shoulder, Consuela added, "Sitting on a' mantelpiece."

He stopped dead, his eyes widening. "Behaviour 'a trifle unpredictable,' indeed!" he muttered.

Entering the dining room with considerable apprehension, he halted, then chuckled. It was a charming room, hung with an exquisite painted Chinese wallpaper. A fine fire burned on the hearth, and the mantel was indeed occupied.

"So you're Milor', are you, sir?" Savage moved nearer, walking slowly, so as not to alarm the very large black Persian cat which sat on the mantel with its tail wrapped about a tall blue and white vase. Savage fancied he knew both the dynasty and the worth of that vase, and his heart failed him when the cat suddenly sprang up and shot one white-tipped paw at a puff of smoke which erupted from the fireplace.

"No!" cried Savage.

The cat turned its head and regarded him. It (also) had a snowy white cravat and its great yellow eyes held a faintly annoyed look as though he had no business interfering in the all important suppression of smoke.

Holding his breath, Savage took another step.

There came a rustle of silks from the hall behind him.

The cat's ears flattened. It sprang from the mantel and shot across the room.

The vase toppled. Groaning, Savage sprang and caught it in the nick of time. "By—God!" he muttered, his knees weak as he clutched it to him.

"Are you fond of porcelains, Mr. Savage?" enquired Mrs. Hythe dryly.

He turned to face her. She had brushed the cobwebs from her hair, but had not changed her green dress, which was now adorned by a stain that had apparently been donated by a tomato. Her spots were no less vivid, and if anything she looked more tired than she had done earlier, but her head was tilted back, and despite the smudge of flour on the end of her nose, there was something regal about her as she met his eyes with that faintly scornful look. Perhaps, he thought, it was because of the way her brows arched, or the disdainful droop to her lips. She had one redeeming feature, at least (in addition to her bosom, which, as he had noticed earlier, was really splendid), her lips were shapely; very much like those of his most recent inamorata, which he had designated "cherry-ripe."

"This," he said, still embracing the vase as he stared at her, "is Ming Dynasty."

She nodded. "I seldom play with it."

Infuriatingly, he felt his face grow hot. "It almost fell," he observed icily.

"Of its own accord, sir?"

Confound the woman! One might imagine her a princess, rather than a spotty landlady with flour on her nose! And come to think of it, this vase—in fact, the entire house—did not equate with near poverty. "Certainly not," he said. About to explain, he paused. He had never much cared for cats, but Helena Hammond's house had been fairly overrun with them, and having become acquainted with The Mushroom, First Cat, Delilah and the rest of the clan, he had developed quite a liking for the creatures. Mrs. Hythe was the type of woman who would slaughter that black cat if she learned of its depravity.

He replaced the vase with reverence, and while doing so took note of the painting which hung above the mantel. "Forgive me for enquiring, ma'am," he drawled, swinging his quizzing glass on its black ribbon. "But is that not a Rembrandt?"

She looked at him steadily. Annoyed, he put up his glass and his brows, and surveyed her.

"I think not," she said, apparently unperturbed by that haughty scrutiny.

He turned his glass to the portrait of the young man looking rather pensively at the greyhound beside him. "Your pardon, ma'am, but I am sure it is a Rembrandt."

"As to *that,* you are correct. Here you are, Barrett. Sit down, dear, and I'll serve dinner."

Elstow took her arm determinedly and ushered her to the head of the table. "You will do no such thing. You look properly hagged, my girl, and I'll wager feel down-pin. *I* shall serve dinner!"

Savage waited until the widow was seated, then took the chair the young man indicated. The wretched woman's obtuse response had been designed to let him know that she did not choose to forgive his impertinence in having dared enquire about the painting. She had evidently taken a pet because she'd caught him, as she imagined, inspecting her silly vase. What did she take him for—some kind of art thief? Well she might sit there like a block of stone until Christmas, for all he cared. He had saved her child, and much thanks he got for it! Certainly, he need not feel obliged to make an effort at polite conversation.

He glanced at her from under his lashes. Her hand trembled as she lifted the water goblet. It was a fine-boned hand, but in need of a manicure. He thought that she looked positively drawn, and felt an irritatingly perverse pang of sympathy. Standing, he went to the sideboard and carried over a decanter of wine.

"Oh," said the widow. "Your pardon. I should have done that."

Silently, he filled her glass.

"No," she said, drawing away as though his touch might contaminate her. "Thank you, but I—"

"Drink it, ma'am," he said firmly. "You need it."

He filled Elstow's glass and his own. When he sat down, Mrs. Hythe was watching him, a wariness in her eyes. They were hazel and red-rimmed. He raised his glass to her. She frowned rebelliously. He said with a quirk of the lips, "I am your paying guest, ma'am. You must humour me."

For a moment longer, she frowned at him. Then, with a sudden and surprisingly engaging smile, she lifted her glass and sipped the wine.

That a lady so burdened with troubles, and doubtless feeling poorly, as Elstow had said, could still manage to smile, won Savage's reluctant admiration, and he began to feel more in charity with the poor creature. Until dinner was served.

Whatever Mrs. Hythe's attributes, cooking was not among them. The vegetables had boiled to a soggy tastelessness; he came near to snapping his knife when he tried to carve his chicken; and the final indignity was suffered when Elstow broke into the raised mutton pie and a piece of pastry rocketed across the table and struck Savage in the eye. Managing to stifle a cry of pain and indignation, he instinctively dabbed at the resultant tears with his napkin, and removed it in time to see the widow's face convulsed with unrepentant and unfeeling amusement. Both she and her cousin proceeded to apologize, but the lady's eyes danced, and her voice was markedly unsteady, while Elstow's mouth twitched in a way that rendered his sincerity questionable. Infuriated, Savage maintained his dignity, which was difficult with crumbs of pastry still smarting in his eye.

When Mrs. Hythe left them to their port and nuts, Elstow excused himself and hurried after her, explaining that she was much too worn out to tidy the kitchen tonight and he must see that she go straight to her bed.

Returning to their guest, Elstow found himself confronted by an aristocrat who greeted all attempts at friendly conversation with a frigid and crushing politeness.

Ten minutes later, Savage rose and wished Mr. Elstow a good-night.

"Good night, sir," said Elstow, standing. And with a timidly hopeful look murmured, "I think I must wash up for poor Primrose before I turn in."

Savage smiled, and without a qualm of conscience, left him to the delights of the kitchen, and retired.

He lay awake for quite some time, thinking decidedly unkind thoughts about the Widow Hythe, and contrasting her primness and belligerence and lack of any redeeming quality (save for her bosom), with the gentle loveliness of Helena Hammond who was now, thanks to his own stupidity, Mrs. Peter Cliveden.

His sleep was disturbed by vivid dreams, which he later attributed to that miserable excuse for a dinner. In one of his dreams he had shrunk to four inches in height and was pursued through the cobwebby and ruined halls of the ancient abbey by the black cat, now covered with white spots. His frantic attempts to elude massive paws equipped with long claws of steel, were reducing him to sobbing exhaustion when, with the cat thundering along only a whisker behind him, he came upon the Ming dynasty vase which was for some reason lying on the floor. He ran inside, retreated to the farthest corner, and cowered there. Two elephantine velvet paws thumped to the vase. Gasping for breath, Savage watched with horrified eyes as a speckled black chin came into view, then a nose and then an enormous eye. His blood ran cold as that great orb scanned him triumphantly. One paw flashed out and crushed his leg so that he could not move. He knew with utter hopelessness that he was about to be dragged forth and played with before he was crunched between the terrible fangs . . .

With a shout, and perspiration dampening his brow, he awoke and started up in bed. The great eye was still there, scant inches from his nose!

For an instant he was paralyzed with horror. Then it was borne in upon him that the eye was now a deep blue; that he was no longer trapped in the vase; and that the weight on his legs was Consuela, who, swamped in his grey coat, was regarding him through his own quizzing glass.

Limp with relief, he slumped back against the pillows. "Oh . . . !" he panted inadequately. And then, reviving somewhat, he sat up. "You repellant little brat! Get off! And give that to me at once!"

Squealing with glee, she scrambled off the bed and danced about, waving his quizzing glass, the long tails of his coat flying out behind her.

Savage, inflamed by righteous indignation, shot from the bed. A piercing yowl, followed by a sharp pain in his bare foot told him he had stepped on Milor's tail. "That'll teach you to chase me round the abbey," he snarled, bravely ignoring his wounded foot as he pursued the elusive sprite who was probably ruining his new coat.

He made a grab for her, but, squeaking, Consuela rolled under the bed. He bent and peered and saw his coattails zipping towards the door. "Come back," he raged, and flung himself over the bed.

Still squealing, she was flying along the hall. He ran three strides, gasping to the chill as his bare feet met the icy floors. His fourth stride terminated on a small and pretty rug. It was also slippery, and for a few seconds he travelled at great speed. The crash when he landed shook the walls and knocked the breath from his lungs. At once, a small face was peering down at him. Anxious eyes scanned him. A cold little hand patted his cheek.

Breathless, but still functioning, he grabbed her. "You little fiend," he panted.

Her laugh trilled out. The quizzing glass was swung up and that great blue eye gleamed at him. He tried unsuccessfully to hold back a wheezing laugh, then managed to get to his feet. With the squealing child under his arm, he marched towards his bed-chamber. "Now, Mistress Mischief," he warned. "You've had your gigs teasing me, but you shall pay!"

Consuela kicked and squeaked with excitement.

Her squeaks were echoed by a shrill scream.

Savage whipped round.

Wearing a gold coloured wrapper that was a cloud of silk and zephyr gauze, the widow watched him, her great hazel eyes dilated with terror. "What are you doing to her?" she shrieked.

"What am *I* doing to *her?*" responded Savage indignantly. He set the child down. "Madam, this revolting—" He broke off. The widow's hazel eyes seemed a trifle less terrified. There was, in fact, a lurking twinkle that put him unpleasantly in remind of her child. His attempt at hauteur was foiled as it burst upon him that he was barefoot and in his nightshirt.

Horrified, he clutched the garment about him and shrank back. Her throaty little chuckle unmanned him. Moaning, he fled.

CHAPTER THREE

SAVAGE'S HOPEFUL LOOK out of the window revealed a sky filled with low-hanging grey clouds and an earth softened by a thick layer of snow. His heart sank. It would be a miracle if he could get the curricle repaired today. He was determined to try, however. Being just as determined not to cower in his room and wait for a tray to be carried up, he tugged on the bellpull. It was bitterly cold and there was no sign of a fire having been set in the grate, or of one having burned here in recent years, and he huddled under the blankets until Elstow arrived a few minutes later, carrying a pannikin of hot water and a towel. He avoided Savage's eyes and said that Mrs. Netty, the housekeeper, was feeling a little improved today and was cooking breakfast. "I trust," he added innocently, as he opened the door, "that you did not hurt your back, sir."

"Do you," said Savage. "Might I enquire as to whether your cousin regards all men as unprincipled animals who interfere with small children? Or am I the only one so suspect?"

Elstow turned to look at him. For a moment the young face was unwontedly stern, then he said coolly, "Consuela is an excessively beautiful child, sir. Perhaps you have noticed. Mrs. Hythe has very good reason to guard her."

Amused, Savage thought, 'So the boy can be top-lofty when he chooses.' And thinking none the worse of him for that quality, he said, "Well, aside from the fact that I'd like to spank the little minx, I've no more evil intentions. I wish you would assure Mrs. Hythe of that fact."

Elstow encountered a whimsical grin. At once his own ingenuous and warm smile flashed, and he promised to do his best. He appeared positively eager to help Savage try to get his curricle repaired. "If worse comes to worst, sir," he said earnestly, "I'm sure Prim would be willing to lend you a saddle."

Convinced that he would be at Whitecaps by sunset, Savage's spirits lifted. Shivering, he shaved and dressed and went downstairs through air that was only slightly less frigid than that in his bedchamber. A fire was burning on the dining room hearth, and the room was fairly comfortable. There was only one cover set, and no sign of the widow or her mischievous daughter, and he sat down feeling rather abandoned.

Mrs. Hythe hurried in almost immediately, carrying a laden tray. Savage came to his feet and took it from her. She looked surprised, and he said suavely,

"Yes, incredible, is it not? But would you believe that I have even been known to say please and thank you?"

"How very gracious," she responded, unruffled. She looked rested, if just as spotty, and her hair was neatly arranged into a coil on her head with small tendrils at the ears. She wore a beige woollen Spencer over a pale lemon muslin gown that he thought quite becoming. Uncovering dishes of eggs, bacon and mushrooms, she apologized for the lack of selection. "I would have sent Barrett to the village," she added, nudging a rack of toasted muffins closer to his hand. "But in view of the weather I hoped you would not object to making do with what we have."

"I do not at all object, for it is ample, ma'am. However, I mean to go into Dingly Dell to arrange for the repair of my curricle, and if there is anything I may bring you, I would be pleased to do so."

She was pouring his coffee and paused to stare at him. "I doubt you will find anyone willing to come out in the snow, Mr. Savage. Especially in this bitter wind."

He smiled. "It is my experience, Mrs. Hythe, that everything has its price."

"Then we must hope that in this particular instance your experience continues to justify your expectations." She finished pouring his coffee while he watched her, not quite knowing what to make of her remark.

He noticed then that although her gown was undoubtedly the creation of a skilled modiste, a seam
of the sleeve was neatly darned and the lace that
edged the low-cut bodice was frayed here and there.
Once again, he was struck by the odd contrast between the magnificent works of art in this house and
the prevailing air of near poverty.

He started as her hand came up to touch her bodice, and he shifted his gaze to find her frowning at
him. Inexplicably, he felt like a schoolboy caught
raiding the jam tarts.

"Your eggs are getting cold, sir," she pointed out
severely.

He thought, 'Perhaps, but my face is not!' "I
was—was wondering, ma'am," he stammered.

"Hmm," she said, as though she knew exactly
what he was wondering, and that it was something
very much to his discredit.

"If you were going to join me," he snapped.

"Thank you, no, sir. I breakfasted hours ago."

Since he had seen her in the upstairs hall less than
an hour since, clad in that very fetching wrapper, this
statement was of doubtful veracity, but before he
could utter a suitably withering comment, she fore-
stalled him by saying hurriedly that she had something for him.

"I will bring it when you have finished," she
added. "Meanwhile, please ring, do you require
anything."

The silver bell she put near his plate was yet another example of exquisite workmanship, the handle cast in the shape of an Elizabethan lady, with the beautifully filigreed bowl forming her skirts. Savage examined it curiously. They could not afford fires in the bedchambers; Mrs. Hythe, obviously well-born, had only one full-time servant and wore threadbare garments; her cousin had given up his studies so as to help her run the property; and she dwelt in a house full of priceless objets d'art. The woman must be wits to let. Even if the objects were of great sentimental value, the sale of only one or two would enable her to live graciously, if not luxuriously. Unless, of course, she had not the right to sell the items. Pondering this, he finished his breakfast and was gazing blindly at his empty cup when he became aware that he was no longer alone.

Consuela stood beside his chair, her big blue eyes fixed solemnly on his face, and with Milor' cleaning himself at her feet. She wore a spotless pinafore over a gown of pink velvet, and a pink velvet ribbon was threaded through her golden curls. Her cheeks were rosy, and a snowflake still clung to one little ringlet. Elstow's remark had been perfectly true: she was a minx, but she was also an excessively beautiful child. It would be a great pity, thought Savage, if she became as spoiled and selfish as many beauties who believed their good looks exempted them from any need to be kind or polite. He fixed her with a steady stare, and was taken aback when she shyly offered him his quizzing glass. Through it, he regarded her unsmilingly.

The long curling lashes swept down, the little head was bowed, then lifted and the great eyes pleaded. "Her bad," she admitted with one of her all encompassing sighs.

"It is not proper for a young lady to enter a gentleman's bedchamber," he pointed out, feeling like a grandfather.

"And her sitted on him."

"Er—yes. Well, that's improper, too."

Another vast sigh, then she said, "Her sorry," and thrust something at him.

Gingerly, he accepted the grey and white feather.

"A fevver," she advised. And with a sudden bright beam, "Her tidied that one, but Milor' et the rest."

With difficulty he muffled an exclamation of repugnance and expressed his thanks.

At once, she spread her skirts and began to dance round the table, singing happily.

Watching her, Savage chuckled, put the surviving feather on the table and wiped his hands on his napkin.

He checked, and the singing stopped as a supple length of tree shoot was placed beside his cup. Mystified, he looked up.

Mrs. Hythe said, "You have the right to chastise my daughter, sir."

"Great heavens, woman! I'm not her papa!"

"Your privacy was invaded, while you were a guest in my house."

"Yes, but—"

"She must learn this is not proper. And I am told you expressed a wish to spank the culprit."

Blast Elstow! "Well, I—"

"Since you were the one abused, you should administer the reprimand. Unless, of course, you do consider such behaviour acceptable."

"Dammitall! You know perfectly—"

Up went her hand in that autocratic gesture again. "Not before the child, if you please, Mr. Savage."

"Oh. Well—Egad! Of course it was not acceptable. But she's only six, and—"

"Consuela is not quite five, sir!"

"Jupiter! There you are, then. One does not strike a child with a da—with a blas—with a curst club, madam!"

The corner of Mrs. Hythe's mouth seemed to twitch for just a second, and two of her spots disappeared into a dimple. "If you feel you should better spank her with your hand, you've my permission."

"I may have *said* I'd like to spank her, but—" He stopped. Mrs. Hythe had whisked herself into the kitchen.

Consuela came to stand beside him.

"A proper bumble-broth you've tripped me into, Mistress Minx," he grumbled.

She picked up the switch and presented it. Blinking tragically at him, she held out her hand. The palm was very small. And it looked soft and pink and defenceless. Savage could all but hear Grandmama's voice: "Every little boy is born a wild creature, and unless somebody cares sufficiently to guide and teach and mold him, he will grow not into an honourable gentleman, but into the kind of ill-behaved monster everyone loathes." Presumably that piece of wisdom applied to little girls also. Tightening his lips, Savage asked, "Do you know why I must spank you, Miss Consuela?"

She nodded. "Him 'spons'ble for her."

"No! Da— Er, no. I am merely an overnight— Oh, the deuce! What I mean is—it is because you were told not to go into the bedchambers of your mama's guests." He brightened hopefully. "Or perhaps your mama forgot to tell you that."

The breath was gathered. "Mama telled her."

"Oh. Then—why did you come and sit on me?"

Mischief danced into her bright face. "Her want to see pastry in his eye."

It was perfectly understandable, after all. When he was a little boy, he'd have— And he would have been spanked. Sighing, he cautioned, "Don't look."

Consuela's eyes shut so tight that her whole face seemed condensed.

He brought the switch down once.

Wailing, she fled.

Considerably demoralized, Savage stamped upstairs and shrugged into his coat. The Spotted Hythe had manoeuvred him into that horrid fiasco. Had any of his friends witnessed it, they'd still be laughing a week from Wednesday. And they'd be justified, for he must be growing a fine crop of dandelions in his brainbox. The week went from bad to worse. He'd be lucky to find his curricle had not been made off with!

Contrary to that dismal thought, however, the curricle was still there, and by the time he and Elstow reached it, a weak sun was peeping through the clouds. The wind had blown the snow into drifts, but on level ground only a few inches had settled. They brushed the snow out of the vehicle before leaving it, and although it was necessary to ride at a slow pace, they had no difficulty in getting to the village.

When they returned in mid-afternoon, Mrs. Hythe came out onto the step to meet them. "I trust your expectations proved justified, Mr. Savage," she called sweetly.

He scowled at her.

Elstow said, "Old Turnbull sent us over to More-or-Less, Prim. Wasn't no use." He sneezed uproariously and, mopping his eyes, went on, "The wheel-wright over there says he'll come when the roads ain't so treacherous. But now it's freezing again, and—

and—" He sneezed again. "Afraid the horses might slip, you see. Matter of fact, mine did."

She gathered her shawl closer and looked at him anxiously. "Yes. I see that you are soaked. You shouldn't have gone jauntering about when you were not quite over your cold." With a vexed glance at Savage she went on, "Not hurt, I hope, Barry?"

"Oh, no," he replied cheerfully. "Just shaken up a trifle."

"Then you must come inside and allow me to put a mustard plaster on your chest. After you have taken care of the horses." Another glance was slanted at Savage.

Clearly, he had been judged and found responsible. Again. Well, he'd not allow the woman the pleasure of seeing how she irritated him. He said breezily, "I'll look after the horses for poor Elstow, ma'am. And then, if you'll let me have my reckoning, I'll take my leave."

Elstow exclaimed, "But I thought you'd decided—"

"Oh, no," interrupted Savage hastily. "I can still reach Portsmouth before dark."

"Hah!" remarked Mrs. Hythe to Milor' who trod daintily past, dragging a large beef bone.

"Sir," Elstow remonstrated, "You must n-not! The roads are very b-bad now."

Mrs. Hythe said, "Barry, your teeth are chattering!" This time, she fixed Savage with a hard stare.

Elstow went on as if she had not spoken. "By the time it s-starts to get dark, and with this beastly wind, they'll surely ice over, and y-you'll be lucky do your cattle not break their knees!"

"Oh, I doubt that," said Savage, with an assurance he did not feel.

"Besides," put in the widow, "you must know, Barry, that everything has its price. If the price of Mr. Savage reaching Portsmouth tonight is that his horses must be shot, he can always buy others, after all."

Elstow's jaw dropped and he stared at her disbelievingly.

Savage's laugh was rather strained, and walking away he wondered how soon her body would be found if he concealed it in the cellars of the old abbey. He had embellished that theme diabolically by the time he left the barn, and he glanced up the hill in faint amusement to where, when they left this morning, he had caught a glimpse of the abbey.

Dark storm clouds hung over the sprawling structure, and the unclad branches of the trees surrounding it looked stark and gloomy. His steps slowed. It really did present a romantic appearance, and so long as he was here... He was climbing the hill almost before he knew it. It did not seem very steep or very far, and he was surprised by the extent of the view when he reached the top of the hill. To the east he could see smoke rising from the village cottages, and a coach was moving at a snail's pace far off on the Portsmouth Turnpike. Only one coach? 'Gad,' he thought. 'The roads must be in a fine state!'

"You must not go there, Mr. Savage!"

Startled, he turned to find the widow coming up behind him, a thick woollen shawl wrapped about her, the ends flying in the wind, and her skirts fluttering. "I have fine horses, ma'am," he said loftily. "I am very sure they will manage to convey me to Portsmouth."

"And you are a famous whip, I understand," she said, out of breath, as though she had been running. "But that is not what I meant, sir. The abbey is unsafe. I must ask that you do not go there."

"Thank you, ma'am, for undertaking this intrepid dash to my rescue. But surely you'll allow me at least a peep inside? It looks to be a fine old place."

"A fine old ruin. Poor thing."

He looked at her curiously. There was sadness in her voice, and her eyes were wistful. Perhaps because the wind had brought roses into her pale cheeks, the spots did not seem so marked. After a minute he asked, "Are you very attached to it?"

Her chin came up. She said with a touch of defiance, "By no means. My father loved it and dreamed of restoring it. He spent a fortune he could ill afford trying to bring it up to style, then a storm wrecked the roof and the rains ruined it again."

"What a pity. It might have been a grand house."

"Yes." She considered him for a moment, then said grudgingly, "Oh—I suppose we can go in, if you will agree to be guided by me, Mr. Savage."

"But of course ma'am. Indeed, I could not ask for a lady more adept at—er, guiding people. Speaking of which," he added as they walked on together, "is your minx of a daughter recovered from the beating I administered—by your conniving?"

"Oh, quite. Are you sir?"

He darted a glance at her. She seemed very innocent, only the dimple was struggling against suppression.

He chuckled. "I'll own I know nothing of small children. I have felt the complete villain all day."

"Pray do not. Consuela is perfectly happy. Indeed, your feeble effort to spank her appears to have earned her sympathy, and she has decided that you want taking care of."

"Very right," he said with a grin. "She is a remarkable child."

"For a minx."

"For a minx. Did you know she gave me a feather, then told me that Milor' had eaten the rest?"

"Oh, my goodness! That little rascal. I hope you threw it away, sir."

"To say truth, I have no wish to start a collection. Still, it was a pretty thought, and prettily done. If she keeps her charm and her looks as she grows up— heaven help the male population!"

He looked at her laughingly, expecting her to be
both pleased and amused, and was surprised to see a
troubled expression. "I meant no offence, ma'am."

"What? Oh, no—no, of course. And I'm afraid
you are right. She will be a great beauty."

Afraid? Surely any mother would be proud that
her daughter was lovely? Of course, Mrs. Hythe was
scarcely a normal woman. She likely thought beauty
was sinful! He responded with a tentative probing,
"Er, dare I ask if you lost her father during the
war?"

"No." She sensed his immediate withdrawal, and
added swiftly, "He died while we were travelling in
Italy. Now be careful of the steps, Mr. Savage. And
please do not wander."

He followed her meekly through a frowning door
that creaked piercingly as she opened it. They entered a huge hall, the cold air smelling of dust and
mould, the light slanting dimly through dirty lat-
ticed windows of which many panes were missing or
broken. At both ends of the room were fireplaces
with gigantic and gloomy chimney pieces that
stretched to the raftered ceiling. A staircase led up to
a gallery that encircled the hall. Everywhere were
signs of damp and decay. He thought, 'The place is
past all hope,' and asked, "Did you live here at any
time, ma'am?"

"When I was small we all lived here. My grand-papa, Papa and my mother, my brother, my sister Katherine...and I."

"It must have required an army of servants. But I fancy your furniture and art collection would have shown to advantage. May we go in there?"

Mrs. Hythe looked uneasily at the door he indicated. "That is the armour hall. You must walk behind me, sir. The abbey has been abandoned for fifteen years. I'd not place much reliance on the safety of the floors, and there are two most grim and grisly cellars below us that are the oldest parts of the building."

"Torture chambers?"

"Yes. And dungeons. Some, at least, although we used it for storage, of course."

She was moving very cautiously. He reached out and took her hand. She jerked it away as though she had been stung, and whirled round to face him. She was suddenly very white, her eyes enormous with fear.

"Good God, madam," he said exasperated. "I have no designs on your virtue, I promise you. I merely was concerned lest you reach the cellars before I do."

She laughed unsteadily. "My—my apologies. You startled me, is all." She stretched out her hand. "I thank you for the thought."

He smiled and took her hand again. But she was shaking and her fingers were like ice, and he wondered whatever had caused her to be so afraid of men.

The armour hall was in a better state than the great hall, and the few broken panes of the lattices had been covered with boards. Old shields and weapons were scattered about the walls or mounted on stands. There were a dozen or more suits of armour and chain mail on display, one of which had fallen to pieces, but the others appearing to be in fairly good condition.

Enthused, Savage exclaimed, "You've some splendid pieces here, ma'am. I've a friend would be overjoyed did you consider parting with any of—"

"No," she said sharply.

"But it seems a shame to let 'em stand here and rust a—"

"We must get back to the cottage."

"Now do not fly into the boughs. I only—"

"I understood you to say you were anxious to leave, Mr. Savage, and it is already past three o'clock."

"Very true. But—just one more room, please. Look, the floor seems in much better case here, and there's not so much dust over by that door. If we—"

"No!" Her voice was almost shrill. She turned away, saying over her shoulder, "You promised!"

"I own it." He followed, reluctantly. Ev Paynton would give his ears for one or two of those suits of armour. He glanced again at the shiny path that led through the dust to the far closed door. There was something in that room the widow did not want him to see. He gave himself a mental shake. And why should that fact be of the least concern to him? To persist would be a fine return for the concession she'd made in bringing him here. Especially when he had already frightened her so badly by holding her hand. He smiled faintly, wondering what she'd do if he took her into his arms and made love to her as he'd made love to Bella, or to the beautiful Dorothea, or— Which was nonsense. He had not the slightest wish to attempt such an experiment, for Primrose Hythe was prim indeed, and was neither pretty nor alluring. Just for a minute, when she'd shrunk from him, he'd thought she had possibilities. There had been something about her eyes, and the way her lips had parted showing her even white teeth... A vision of his matchless Helena came into his mind. He sighed faintly, and followed the widow into the icy teeth of the wind.

She walked so rapidly that he had his work cut out to keep up with her, and called a warning against proceeding at such speed over the snow, which, having partially melted and then frozen again, was little more than a sheet of ice.

"I am worried about Barrett," she replied. "He had a very bad case of chicken pox and was not completely over it when he was chilled yesterday. He knows he is susceptible to inflammations of the lungs, but I can never get him to wear a scarf and he forgets his gloves half the time. He should not have gone out in this bitter wind today, much less have stayed out so long."

"You mean, I think, that *I* should not have kept him out for so long, madam?"

"Just so."

"Nonsense. He is a man, not a child."

"All men are children," she said coldly. "At least—all nice men a—" She slipped, and the words ended in a shriek.

Savage grabbed for and caught her, only to slip himself and let out a shout as they skidded for some distance down the hill.

Laughing helplessly, he sat up, the widow still clasped in his arms. "At least we came...down faster than we...went up," he gasped.

For the first time since he'd met her, she looked like a young girl, with her unaffected laughter and her big eyes bright and sparkling. Out of breath, she said with an exaggeratedly mournful air, "But at what...cost to...our dignity!"

"Never mind about dignity—admit that whatever I lack, I make a famous toboggan."

She laughed again. "Poor soul, you took the brunt of the disaster. You must be soaked through. I hope you have taken no hurt?"

"None. For a fallen woman, Mrs. Hythe, you weigh very little and—"

The merriment faded from her face. As if suddenly becoming aware that she sat on his lap and that his arms were around her, she pulled away. "Oh, heavens! How improper this is."

"Yes," he agreed, making no move to free her. "And I have frightened you again. Why? If it is because I called you a fallen woman, I referred to our small disaster, nothing more."

He frowned then, for the bright colour had left her cheeks and she was beginning to tremble again.

"Let me go—please," she said in a small, quivering voice.

"Of course. If you will answer one question that I'll admit I've no right to ask." She turned her head away but said nothing. He went on, "Mrs. Hythe—did your husband treat you ill?"

"No."

"But—he *is* dead?"

She nodded, then said with an unexpected twinkle, "What is your drama, sir? That I was married to an evil bluebeard who beat me for breakfast and supper?"

"Yes. And who has forbidden you to sell off some of your treasures."

"On pain of instant throttling."

"And who even now lurks in your great abbey, which is the reason you would not let me go into that third room just now, for you knew he would have my throat cut in the wink of an eye."

She said, laughing, "What a delicious tale of horror, but I promise you, Mr. Savage, there is not a word of truth in it."

"Will you also promise me that you are not frightened of something—or someone?"

She stiffened, then said brightly, "You demanded one question, sir, and have stolen another, at the very least. Now you must keep your word and help me—" Her eyes became very wide. She gave a little gasp and clutched his hand tighter.

"What is it? Have you hurt yourself, ma'am?"

"Just—a little. My ankle. I must have twisted it, but—if you will help me..."

He was already lifting her aside, and he scrambled to his feet and bent to take both her hands. Her attempt to stand was gallant but in vain. Watching her pale face and twitching mouth, he swept her up.

"No!" she cried. "Pray set me down, sir. I—I can manage."

"We'll see that when I get you home." He smiled into her scared eyes. "Now do try not to wriggle, ma'am, or I'll likely capsize us again."

When they approached the house, Consuela came dancing out to meet them, her little cloak flying. Her delighted giggles ceased when Savage asked her to fetch her cousin, and she realized that this was not a game. "Mama...?" she whimpered, her eyes huge with sudden fear as she clutched the hand Mrs. Hythe stretched out to her. "Mama?"

"It's all right, darling. Mama slipped on the snow and has turned her ankle a little, that's all."

Those great blue eyes flew to Savage.

He said, "Never mind about your mama. Have a care for me. I am very frightened, for I have never tended a sick lady. Will you help me, Miss Consuela?"

She watched him for a moment, then the beaming smile dawned. She patted her mother's knee and ran to open the kitchen door. "Her help, Mr. Avid."

The widow gave a muffled snort. Savage groaned. "You may call me Mr. Leo," he suggested. "Easier. Now run and find Mr. Barrett Elstow."

She nodded and it was evidently necessary that she come to pat Savage's knee also. "Her find Brettoe."

"Oh—no, pray do not," said Mrs. Hythe distressfully. "I sent him up to lie down upon his bed, Mr. Savage. He has a very nasty cough."

"Well, it won't kill him to come down for a minute or two. Run along, Consuela."

Carrying the widow into the withdrawing room, Savage deposited her upon the salmon brocade sofa. He heard her gasp as he set her down, and he shrugged out of his driving coat and asked irritably, "Will your housekeeper be able to help?"

"No, no. Netty is no longer young, and far from well. She was obliged to return to her bed after luncheon. But pray do not be anxious for me. I am sure I will be all right." She looked up at him imploringly. "I'll just rest here for a little while. Oh, dear, you are soaked! And good gracious—look at the time! Mr. Savage, you must be on your way, or you will never reach Portsmouth tonight."

He should indeed be on his way, but it was damn near freezing in here, and the wretched woman must make things worse by denying that she was in pain, and making no least demand of him, or indulging in vapours and tears as any normal female would do. He said gruffly, "I'll build up the fire at least, before I leave."

"Thank you. You are very good."

She spoke calmly, but when he turned from having set a blaze crackling around the logs he'd piled on the fire she had managed to ease out of her half-boot and stocking and was looking dismayed. He walked over to inspect the injury. Her foot was daintily formed but the ankle was already swollen and starting to discolour.

He said, "I fear it is at the least a strain, Mrs. Hythe, but we should have an apothecary out here to look at it. If it should be sprained—"

"It *must* not be," she cried, tears gemming on her lashes as she looked up at him. "I cannot be ill! I *cannot!* Who ever will—" She bit her lip, then said, blinking hard, "But we will manage, never fear. Your reckoning is on the desk in the kitchen. I am most embarrassed to ask it of you, but if you could possibly stop for just a minute at the village, Mr. Turnbull will arrange for the apothecary to come out to us. I want him to look at Barrett."

He growled, "You would do well to think of yourself for once, ma'am," and stamped into the kitchen.

He was counting out the payment when Elstow came in, coughing. "I say, what beastly luck." The cough sounded tight and harsh. "Prim says you fell too, sir. The hill can be treacherous in the snow." Another cough, which he obviously fought to mute.

Savage glared at him. The fine young face was pale except for the patches of colour high on the cheek-bones, and the eyes had a slightly dulled look. "I decided to have a look at the abbey," said Savage, keeping his voice low. "Mrs. Hythe was kind enough to take me through."

Elstow looked astonished. "Prim took you—*inside?*"

"Why not?" Deviously, he said, "It looks sturdy enough."

"Oh, yes. The upstairs rooms are badly water damaged, but the ground floor's safe enough."

Savage could almost hear Mrs. Hythe cautioning,
"You must walk behind me... I'd not place much
reliance on the safety of the floors..."

Elstow was saying, "What did you think of all the
armour? Jolly splendid, isn't it?"

"Yes. I've a friend would pay a pretty penny to
buy some of the pieces. Do you fancy your cousin
could be persuaded to sell?"

Elstow started to speak then coughed again and
asked in a wheezy voice, "Is that all you were able to
see? None of the other rooms?"

"Only the one next to the armoury."

"Good God! She let you see—" But he was again
interrupted by the cough that he could not seem to
stop until Savage had forced him into a chair and
thrust a glass of water into his hand.

After a few mouthfuls he managed a grin, although he looked wan and exhausted. "Thank you,
sir. What do you want us to do about your curricle?"

"I'll send one of my grandmama's people to repair it. Is there anyone in the village who can come
out here and help for a day or two? Your housekeeper is not to be disturbed, I take it. No—" he
flung up one hand "—do not talk. Whisper."

"Netty was Prim's nurse, you see. She should have
been retired years since, but...she's a dear old thing,
and feels needed. Prim says that's important when
one is elderly. Miss Faith Underhill, the... the vi-

car's daughter, might come. She helped before when Uncle John—Prim's father—died.''

"Very good. I'll see what I can arrange." And feeling the ultimate cad, Savage asked, "What about food? Have you sufficient?''

"Never you fear, sir. We shall do splendidly. And thank you for all your help.''

"Not at all.''

Consuela came dancing in and seized him by the leg. "Him tell her story.''

Elstow said gently, "Mr. Savage has to go to his own home, sprout. I'll tell you a story. Later.''

The blue eyes lifted tragically to Savage's face.

He could see the tears in them, all the way to Dingly Down.

CHAPTER FOUR

"THE FACT that one has seen 'em all one's life," muttered Savage, "don't mean one knows how to deal with the confounded articles."

From some dim recess of memory he called up a picture of his father's chef knocking two together and emptying the contents into a dish. "Simple enough," he said. "Not going to explode, after all."

He put the theory into practice, roared an exasperated "God—bless it!" and ignored Consuela's shrieks as he gingerly picked eggshell from his right ear. He'd washed his hands, which had been well coated with soot from his battle with the various fires, but it became apparent that he must wash them again. He pumped icy water into the bowl and washed as rapidly as possible, then towelled his hands hard in an effort to get the blood circulating again.

"You want for conduct," he advised Consuela severely. "And I'll have you know it ain't polite for a lady to roll about on the floor. Instead of all that noise you might better tell me how your mama opens these blas—these miserable contraptions."

Sobbing, she climbed to her feet, opened a drawer, and handed him a knife. "Mama use this."

"She *cuts* 'em open?"

His doubts proved well justified, but Milor' was perfectly willing to clean up the floor.

Moaning, Consuela dried her eyes. "No. Him hit it," she advised weakly.

"I'd like to damned well beat it to a pulp," he muttered through his teeth, but since he had to an extent already done so, he complied. His first attack deposited a piece of shell on the ceiling, but by means of some very fast juggling he caught part of the yolk as it slithered over the side of the table and, encouraged, told Consuela that he was "getting the hang of it" now.

Half an hour later, he carried up the tray, and found Mrs. Hythe, pale but triumphant, sitting on the side of the bed, fully dressed.

"How did you manage that?" he demanded, putting the tray on a small table by the windows.

"I can hop," she said. "And if I can prevail upon you to find Papa's walking cane, I will do very well." She looked at brown and curling eggs and charred toast, and said nobly, "Oh, sir! You are too good."

"Her make a' toast," bragged Consuela.

Mrs. Hythe hugged her. "Did you, darling? What a good helper. Mr. Savage, there is no need for you to carry my tray up here. If you could just assist me downstairs, I—"

"Madam," he said. "That cloth-headed apothecary told you yesterday that the ankle will mend *if*
you rest. I have made you breakfast in bed, and
breakfast in bed you will have." He picked her up,
deposited her against the pillows and pulled the covers over her.

"It looks lovely," she exclaimed, blushing quite
prettily. "But I fear you have been put to a great deal
of trouble."

"Pish," said Savage.

"Her bringed him more eggs," advised Consuela.

The widow looked surprised. "But there were a
dozen and—"

"Er, I broke one. Or, er, two," he admitted.

"One goed on a' ceiling," said Consuela, her eyes
sparkling.

The widow's jaw dropped.

Savage said briskly, "Come along Mistress Traitor. We've to take trays to your cousin and Mrs.
Netty."

Mrs. Hythe said, "No, really, Mr. Savage. I cannot let you wait on us. You must get to Portsmouth,
and—"

"Roads are absolutely impassable, ma'am, and
they won't take me in the village, so you're doomed
to endure me for a day or two."

"*Endure* you! Sir, if you but knew how grateful I
am. Had you not come back to us—" She remembered her unspeakable relief when he had ridden in

again yesterday afternoon, bringing the apothecary with him, and her lips trembled.

Savage said hurriedly, "Had I not insisted upon your taking me up to the abbey, you'd not have fallen. Further, as you have repeatedly informed me, I am responsible both for Elstow's illness and for littering England with broken-kneed hacks."

Distressed, she faltered, "No—really, I am a wretch if I implied—"

"Yes, you are. And you did."

She bit her lip, and her eyes fell.

Lifting her chin with one long finger, he said, "My grandmama, who is a most exasperatingly wise lady, once told me that the worst thing you can do to those who treat you ill is to repay them with kindness. There is nothing will make 'em angrier."

The twinkle in his blue eyes restored the smile to her face. She said, "And that is what you are doing to me, is it, Mr. Savage?"

"Exactly so, and you'd not believe how smug it makes me feel. Now, I am a very busy man and cannot be loitering about ladies' bedchambers when there is work to be done." He took the silver bell from his pocket and placed it on her tray. "If you need anything, please ring."

She gave an embarrassed laugh. "You quite put me to the blush, sir."

"And a very charming blush it is."

"Now *that,*" she said, "was an excellent hit!"

He grinned, and went out with Consuela dancing along beside him.

During the two days that followed, Mr. Leopold Savage worked harder than he had ever worked in his life. Mrs. Netty, the "housekeeper" was a frail and elderly lady with crimped grey hair and a humorous mouth, who he rather suspected was thoroughly enjoying watching a male member of the Quality toil from dawn to dusk. Elstow, on the other hand, was really ill, and although he made light of his hacking cough, his high colour and the burning heat of his skin worried Savage. The apothecary had pursed his lips and pronounced that Mr. Elstow merely suffered a feverish cold. He'd left a draught, and ordered complete rest, but Savage wished he could summon his grandmother's competent, if toad-eating, physician from Portsmouth, to look at the boy.

True to her word, Mrs. Hythe insisted that she be carried downstairs in the mornings, and although he would not permit this until he had lit the fires, he was greatly relieved to have the benefit of her instruction.

He had been unable to hire help in the village, most of the inhabitants either having family members who had not as yet had chicken pox, or being reluctant to journey to the abbey in such bad weather. The vicar, however, a kindly and sympathetic gentleman, had promised that as soon as his spinster daughter was able to return from Winchester, where she visited her aunt, she would come to Erskine Abbey daily, for as long as she was needed.

Meanwhile, with blithe inefficiency Savage and Consuela did the washing up, made pots of tea, trudged up and down stairs with trays and hot water for the invalids, fed the chickens, banked the fires, and shared conversations that were often incomprehensible to one or other of them. Savage tended the horses and followed the widow's instructions as to meals. At the end of the day, having told Consuela a bedtime story and tucked her into bed, carried Mrs. Hythe to her room, and looked after Elstow and Mrs. Netty, he practically fell into his own bed and slept the sleep of the just.

Cooking presented his worst challenge, and there were some truly gruesome meals. The first day he contrived to set fire to a frying pan, allowed the potatoes to boil over, and had to cook the mutton chops again when the insides were found to be raw. Somehow, the disasters all turned to laughter, and nobody starved. The second day he did a little better, but it was a day not free of problems in other respects.

It was brought to the attention of the humans at dinner time that Milor' had wandered into territory he might better have avoided. Savage noticed Mrs. Hythe looking about in a puzzled way, and at first supposed her to be disenchanted with the aroma of

his culinary efforts. Very soon however, his own nose
was wrinkling, and when they sat down to table,
Consuela—allowed during these difficult days to stay
up and eat with the adults—said an uninhibited,
"Oh, pooh!"

Mrs. Hythe clapped a napkin to her dainty nose,
and Savage groaned. "Is it that cat? It must go out!"

Milor' having been ejected, and several candles
wafted about the room, they were able to eat their
dinner. Savage took Consuela up to bed, tended to
Elstow's needs and brought down his and Mrs. Netty's trays. When he came into the kitchen, he was
irked to discover the widow clinging to a chairback
with one hand while she attempted to wash up with
the other.

"Desist, Spotted Hythe," he commanded.

"Oh! What an unkind appellation," she protested. "And I shall certainly not desist. Can you
imagine how it makes me feel to fall deeper into your
debt with each day that passes?"

She squealed as he picked her up bodily, and sat
her on the chair. "I should imagine you would be
overset with gratitude, and yearning to repay me."

She looked at him with a trace of unease.

"Whereby you may dry," he said, bowing as he
presented her with the towel.

"Oh." She kept her eyes downcast as he wrapped
another towel about himself.

"You may well avoid my eye," he scolded. "You were at your melodrama-ing, again."

"Indeed I was not. And there is no such word as melodrama-ing."

"Then there should be, for it perfectly describes the fact that you took my innocent remark and twisted it so as to believe I was going to offer you a pretty little flat in Town, conveniently adjacent to mine own."

She blushed, and scrubbed vigorously at the plate he handed her. "It would be exceeding improper for a lady to know that London beaux make such offers."

"The lady who does not know it, must be a widgeon, and I do not take you for a widgeon, ma'am."

"And you will not take me for—" In the nick of time she halted what would have been a flagrantly bold remark.

He prompted silkily, "For what—Mrs. Primrose?"

It was the first time he had spoken her given name. She felt flustered and fought to preserve her countenance. "For a blind goose, sir. You are teasing me to try and put me off, but despite what you say, I know you *could* have left us, save that your kind heart kept you here."

He stared at her for a minute, then gave a whoop of laughter. "I wish some of my friends might have heard me described as having a kind heart. Most of them would tell you I have no heart at all.''

"In which case you know a set of blockheads, sir. And you are worrying about Barrett, I think.''

Her expression was grave, but she also had a worn look. He said, "I am concerned about *you*, ma'am. I have yet to hear you complain, and you think only of others, but I believe that foot is paining you. We must put some ice on it. Lord knows there's plenty to hand.''

"Or to foot,'' she said whimsically.

He chuckled. "Just so. As to your cousin, I'll administer his medicine after I get you tucked up for the night.''

"But you think the medicine is not helping him. No—do not tell me I am melodrama-ing again. I can read it in your eyes. You think he is very ill!''

"And up she goes into the boughs again! Barrett Elstow is a healthy young fellow who merely chances to have caught a feverish cold, but that will not do for your sense of the dramatic! You prefer to have him languishing with the pneumonia!''

"Heaven forbid! But—''

He touched her hand, and said very gently, "Ma'am, I promise you. If the cough isn't improved by tomorrow, I'll fetch the apothecary. Meanwhile, I shall venture boldly into the arctic wastes to gather some ice.''

When he opened the back door however, Milor' darted in, eluding the hand that snatched for him.

"Oh, dear," moaned the widow. "Whatever are we to do, sir? We cannot keep him out all night, or he will surely freeze."

"Then we shall have to lock him in here. Perhaps he'll manage to clean himself. Cats are very fastidious, you know."

"I hope so," said Mrs. Hythe, trying not to breathe deeply.

"If not," said Savage, "I'll give him a bath tomorrow morning."

Rather faintly, she echoed, "Give him a ... bath? You never would!"

"Why would I not? Consuela was but now telling me that she and Elstow bathed him a few months ago, for—er, similar reasons."

"Oh! That little rascal! Milor' had only just taken us on then, as it were, and was in terrible condition. But, in fact—"

"Mrs. Hythe, allow me to point out—item: we are not able to keep the creature in the barn, where, I might add, it belongs. Item: human beings require to breathe. Item: unless you give me permission to skin the repuls—er, the animal, steps must be taken."

"Yes, yes. But you do not understand. Barrett has a very great kindness for animals, but—"

At once a saturnine look dawned. He drawled, "Whereas I, *au contraire,* decapitate a cat an hour with my trusty hatchet."

"Mr. Savage, pray do not be foolish. I know you are not unkind, but you *are* widely held to be a man of fashion, and—"

"By Gad, madam! Never hide your teeth! Name me a dandy and have done!"

"If you will but let me—"

He threw up one hand in the autocratic gesture that never failed to irk her. "There is no more to be said. While I am prepared to believe that your cousin is a cat washer par excellence, I think I am not incapable of equalling his accomplishments. Milor' is a small animal, and I am a strong and determined man. There is no contest."

In this particular instance, Mr. Leopold Byrne Savage was absolutely correct.

CONVINCED BY THE SOUNDS from belowstairs that bloody murder had been done, Barrett Elstow set his breakfast tray aside, dragged himself up in bed, and was reaching for his dressing gown when his bedroom door burst open.

A bedraggled and berserk apparition rushed to look under the bed, fling open the doors of the wardrobe, and roar, "Where is she? Are you protecting the little witch? By George, but I'll find her! Never think I won't!"

Looking from the puddled floor to his drenched visitor, Elstow shrank back against the pillows and pointed out uneasily, "You are very—wet, sir."

"And there's a perspicacious remark, if ever I heard one!" A corner of his mind noting with relief that Elstow looked less feverish today, Savage dashed soapsuds from one eyebrow, and snarled, "You may be sure I am wet! And you are to blame, repellant youth! Why the *devil* did you not warn me? Where *is* the brat, I say?"

"If you mean Consuela, I don't know, but— Good God! Your face!"

Savage glanced in the mirror at the three long red lines that scored his right cheek, and at his wet and wild appearance. "My face," he moaned, wiping more soapsuds from the end of his nose. "I marvel I still have one! And only look at my hands!"

Barrett inspected the gouged and bloodied victims, and raised his eyes in awe to the fuming paying guest/cum nurse/cum general factotum. "Oh—no," he half-whispered. "Leo...you—you never gave Milor' a bath?"

"Do not look at me with sympathy *now*, blast your ears! Why didn't you warn me yesterday that the confounded animal has sixteen legs and a hundred razors concealed about its mangy carcass?"

His mouth twitching, Elstow lay back against the pillows and said unsteadily, "If—you had but...mentioned it to me."

"I did not *mention* it because that devious child implied it was an easy task and one you had easily managed. After all I have done! 'Ingratitude, where is thy sting?'—or however that goes." Unmanned, Savage sank onto the edge of the bed and used a corner of the sheet to dab at his dripping hair. "When first I put the brute into the tub," he said mournfully, "it raised no objection."

"But when you started to apply the soap—"

"It went *berserk!* Dammitall! When it wasn't trying to sink its beastly fangs into my arm, it was clawing my face! And when I put a stop to that, it gouged me with its back feet. Both at once! And that was but the beginning!"

"You—you should have let him go," gulped Elstow.

"Let him *go?* Are you mad? I did not dare! He was ready to hurl himself at my throat!"

"How..." choked out Elstow, "did you escape?"

"He jumped over me when I chanced to fall." Savage explored his hip broodingly. "Instead of lying here listening to it all," he added, "you might better have investigated. I know you're unwell, but were I on my deathbed and heard the kind of demoniac noise that blasted brute was emitting, I'd have come to the aid of my fellow man, I can tell you!"

"What... about Prim? Could she n-not have..."

Savage stood. He said bitterly, "The Spotted Hythe was much too busy pointing out that I am a strong and determined man, and Milor' is a small animal."

"If you called my cousin that," sighed Elstow, wiping his eyes, "I don't wonder she wouldn't help."

"Well, I did, and I'm jolly glad I made a small score, for she didn't like it above half, for all it's perfectly apt."

"No, it isn't. Prim's spots are almost gone."

"At all events, I wish her joy of the ocean in the kitchen. I assure you I ain't going to clean it up!"

Savage's dream of retribution was foiled, however, for when he went downstairs some half-hour later, having changed his clothes and to an extent dried his hair, he heard feminine laughter emanating from the kitchen. He walked in with as dignified an air as he could summon, and found that a plump and comely young damsel with golden curls and china blue eyes was using a towel to mop up the floor.

Mrs. Hythe, markedly unrepentant, introduced her as Miss Faith Underhill, who had been so kind as to come and help them.

The vicar's mention of his "spinster daughter" had somehow prepared Savage for a gaunt, middle-aged lady, not for this pretty girl with her properly shy manner. He bowed, and very conscious of the mischief in Mrs. Hythe's face, said that Miss Underhill's assistance would be much appreciated.

"It does seem, sir," she said, dropping him a curtsy, "that I have come at an opportune moment. Indeed, when first I arrived I thought Consuela had been playing in here."

"She was, ma'am," said Savage, dourly.

"Good gracious," exclaimed Mrs. Hythe, inspecting him narrowly. "You are badly scratched, sir. You must permit that I attend to your poor face."

Miss Underhill brought the medical supplies, then hurried off to see what she could do for Mrs. Netty and Elstow.

"Sit here, by me, Mr. Savage," said the widow. "I am so glad Faith could come. She is an excellent nurse, and the kindest creature. Turn your face this way a little, if you will."

She applied salve to his scratches with great concentration, her lips a little parted as she leaned to him. She had chosen a gown of light golden linen today, which seemed to deepen the golden flecks in her hazel eyes. They were kinder eyes than she had shown him when he first arrived, and watching them he wondered absently if she was less afraid of him. His gaze drifted lower. Jove, but the widow had a magnificent—

"I said, please close your eyes for a moment," she repeated, her dimple peeping again.

"Oh." Irritated by a foolish and quite unwarranted sense of guilt, he obliged, and thus became more aware of the sweet fresh scent of her. "Do you intend to treat my other wounds also, ma'am?"

"Other wounds . . . ?"

He lifted his hands and she uttered a gratifyingly concerned exclamation.

"Good Gad," cried a tenor voice from the back door. "Shall I go away again, dear boy?"

His eyes alight, Savage sprang to his feet. "Pay! Deuce take me, but I'm glad to see you! However did you find me?"

The young Corinthian who came into the room wore a long drab coat, which reached almost to his ankles and was adorned with so many capes that he looked almost square. A high crowned beaver hat was set at a jaunty angle on his brown hair, and a thick woollen scarf was wrapped about his throat. His clean-cut face was illumined by a warm smile as he rather gingerly shook hands with his friend, and his grey eyes, having alighted upon the widow, returned to her with great frequency.

"Sent down by your sire with an urgent message," he said. "You drove off to see Lady Carlotta, says he, before he learned that her ladyship ain't at Whitecaps. He fancied you'd choose to stay there since you and he—er . . ."

"Yes, quite. So he sent you to tell me to come back, eh?" Noting that his friend's attention wandered, Savage exclaimed, "Gad, and I'm a clod! Mrs. Hythe, pray allow me to present Sir Everard Paynton. Pay, this poor lady is Mrs. Primrose Hythe. Who is no longer contagious, I might add."

Bowing with graceful gallantry over the widow's hand, Sir Everard said, "Whatever you suffered, ma'am, I'd be most happy to catch it!"

Savage struggled without marked success to muffle a snort of mirth at what he considered a most fatuous remark.

Mrs. Hythe, however, smiled upon the new arrival. "I hope you will take tea with us, Sir Everard. Or perhaps you can stay to luncheon?"

"If he does," inserted Savage indignantly, "I don't propose to wear myself to a shade preparing it!"

Paynton looked at him as if he'd taken leave of his senses, but Mrs. Hythe said with saintly humility, "But of course not, sir. You are quite free of such odious tasks now that Miss Underhill has come to us."

"Oh," said Savage.

"Odious tasks...?" echoed Paynton, curious. "Jehosophat, Leo! What the deuce happened to your face? Have you been pursuing—" He broke off with a gasp of mortification, turned very red, and concentrated upon removing his coat and hat and handing them to Savage.

"Dolt." Savage tossed the garments carelessly onto a chair. "I'd an encounter with a wildcat, but never mind about that. How did you find me? I never reached Whitecaps."

"So I discovered, dear boy. Gave me a bit of a turn. There have been some nasty spills along the turnpike, you see, Mrs. Hythe, and I know how Leo drives."

"The devil!" exclaimed Savage. "If you came to make snide remarks and be a misery, you may take yourself off again! I've had enough of misery since I came here!"

"I say!" Paynton looked shocked. "Not polite, Leo! Jolly impolite, in fact!"

"Never worry, sir," said the widow, her eyes downcast. "Poor Mr. Savage has indeed grounds for complaint, and he has been more than kind." Reaching for her cane, she started to struggle to her feet. "I'll prepare tea."

"No, no!" Paynton fairly sprang to swing the trivet so that the kettle would boil. "I am wholly at your service." His glance again slanted to Savage's clawed face, and he asked with rather a grim look, "Had you an—er, accident, ma'am?"

"She fell on the ice," said Savage, bristling. He marched with a proprietary air to take out the tea caddy and elbow his friend aside as Paynton attempted a move towards the china cabinet. "And before you decide, Pay, that I have committed heaven knows what heinous crimes, you'd best tell me where you had word of me."

"Why, from a constable who was supervising the removal of a tree from the turnpike." Paynton neatly commandeered the chair beside the widow that Savage had vacated. "And then from a stablehand in a quaint hamlet called More-or-Less. He said you was there trying to get your wheel repaired. Split, did it? Not surprised. Best come back to Town with me, dear boy."

"Is that the sum total of your urgent message, Pay?"

Paynton, who was watching Mrs. Hythe's graceful hands as she arranged the teacups, murmured, "Mmmm." The widow's dimple appeared and from under her lashes she slanted an amused glance at him.

Savage noted that coquettish look and wondered that his friend was not appalled by it, even though one must admit that the widow's lashes were very long, and curled rather charmingly.... He snapped, "Then you are at liberty to go back."

"Eh? What? Oh—the message. No, dear boy. It is that your sire and your grandmama have put their heads together and—" He checked, glancing from Savage to the widow uncertainly.

"I am sure you would wish to be private, gentlemen." Mrs. Hythe managed to rise to her feet. "And I must see where Consuela is gone to. Pray excuse me."

Both men stood as she limped out, and Paynton made a mad dash to open the door for her. Closing it, he turned to his friend, shaking his head, his eyes admiring. "Might have known you'd find yourself a perch with an Incomparable, dear boy!"

"What it is, Paynton," said Savage unequivocally, "the porridge that fills your brainbox has frozen solid."

"And I suppose," murmured Sir Everard, strolling back to his chair, "that those scratches are not the result of your attempting to—"

"No, damn you! They are not! I told you I'd an encounter with a wild *cat* and I didn't mean a wild widow! I've not the faintest interest in Mrs. Primrose Hythe. I merely chance to be humanitarian enough to be sorry for the woman. No more, and no less."

Sir Everard inspected one cuticle. "Hmm. I recall your once telling me that all widows are willing...so I—"

"Not this one, blast you! And don't forget it!"

"But—dear boy—if you've no interest in her, you must not be a dog-in-the-manger, you know. Not like you, Leo. No, really!"

Savage stamped over to stand before his friend, hands on hips and a dangerous glint in his eye. "I shall ask you for the fourth time, Paynton—what is this urgent message?"

"Oh, yes. Well, gird thy loins, my lad. It seems
your father and Lady Carlotta are going to give a
ball. In March."

Savage curled his lip and sneered, "Jove, but you
terrify me! Is that all?"

"And they have sent out invitations to the fairest
among the ton, my poor fatted calf."

Savage stared at him. "Do you . . . say . . . ?"

"That you are to be there—on pain of death—and
choose your mate." Watching his friend's choleric
countenance with eyes alight with amusement,
Paynton murmured, "'Twould seem, my tulip, that
your bachelor days are done."

"WELL, SHE AIN'T abovestairs," said Savage, coming into the kitchen where the widow sat shelling
peas. "Why are you doing that? I had thought Miss
Underhill came to perform the menial tasks."

The widow shook her head at him and the ribbons that hung behind her dainty cap danced with
her curls. "Faith is a family friend," she pointed out.
"She has come to help nurse Barrett and poor Mrs.
Netty—"

He gave a scornful grunt. "Poor Mrs. Netty being as well as you or I but enjoying her imaginary
infirmities. And at all events, Miss Faith ain't tend-
ing either of our invalids. Did Paynton frighten her
away?"

"Certainly not. They have gone out together to look for Consuela. And to say truth, I fancy Sir Everard finds Faith most attractive."

"Does he so? Well, *now* he shows a spark of sense." His scowl lightening, he said. "I'd best go and shovel some more coal."

"No need, Mr. Savage. Your friend was so kind as to do so whilst you were upstairs, and with not the least hint of condescension." She smiled. "*Such* a considerate gentleman."

"I should like to know who the devil asked him to interfere! I had it all arranged just as I like it!"

The widow's hands stilled, and she turned her head to stare at him. "You had the *coal* arranged?"

"What's so dashed odd about that? You are rather short, as a matter of fact, and I've divided it out so as to last until we can get the coal merchant to come."

"How very tidy of you," she said admiringly. "I shall do well to study your methods."

"Well, you will," he said, eyeing her meekness with some suspicion. "Tidiness is next to Godliness, so 'tis said, and I'll own I'm a great one for neatness and order."

"Are you sure, sir?"

His scowl returned, drawing down his brows and bringing the angry glint back into his blue eyes. "What the devil d'you mean by that?"

"I had thought," she said, all innocence, "that the word used was 'cleanliness' not 'tidiness'."

"Six of one, half a dozen of another. You split hairs, ma'am."

As if impelled by the word, her eyes lifted to his dark head. She lowered them at once and said nothing, but the dimple in her cheek was in evidence. As he watched, it seemed to become more marked rather than quickly vanishing. And he realized with a distinct shock that it was spot-less.

He fairly pounced to seize her by the chin and jerk her head up, thus surprising a look of mischief before it was replaced by annoyance. "Where are your chicken pox?" he demanded.

She slapped his hand away. "I took them off when I saw Sir Everard coming."

"I shouldn't wonder." His mouth twisted with cynicism. "A dashed good catch is Paynton."

Her eyes flashed and a flood of angry colour lit her pale cheeks. Seizing her cane, she stood, facing him. He did not retreat, but his dark head tossed a little higher and he watched her with a proud and icy hauteur.

Suddenly, the widow laughed merrily. "Foolish man," she cried. "My nasty spots faded away and were gone yesterday, had you but eyes to see. And do pray disabuse your mind of any notion that I seek a new husband. I do not, I promise you!"

His hands shot out and gripped her shoulders. Pulling her close to him, he growled, "I may be a foolish man, but I am not quite blind, madam. I saw how you fluttered your lashes at Paynton. Blew up a regular gale!"

"It is no concern of yours if I flutter my lashes at the dustman! Let me go at once!"

Instead, he wrenched her closer so that the cane fell. "If you don't want a husband there's no call for you to flutter your lashes at anyone."

She blinked up at him. His hands were very strong and his mouth looked so grim, but the anger had gone from his eyes. They held a softness. Almost, a tenderness . . . Resistless, she allowed herself to sway towards him. His lips curved into the smile that was so charming, so transforming. Fighting for common sense, she managed, "Whatever . . . made you so angry that you must strike out at everyone?"

Memory, and reason, flooded back. Savage jolted, and the dreaming smile vanished. "My father and my grandmama have united to provide me a bride." He guided her back into the chair and picked up her cane. "If ever I heard of such rank interference in a fellow's life."

Her breathing a little uneven, she said, "It does sound rather highhanded. Is there no lady you favour, sir?"

"If there was, I'd make a bolt to Gretna Green with her, and confound the pair of 'em!"

"Which would be very foolish," she pointed out, "since it would disgrace you both *and* distress your families."

Paying no need to this sensible observation, he picked up a pea and began to tear it to shreds with quick angry movements. "They mean to give a ball, invite all the fairest in the land, and I'm to select the winning candidate!"

"Good gracious! Are you *so* much sought after, Mr. Savage?"

Her astonishment added fuel to the fire of his rage. "Surprising, ain't it?" His smile now was not pleasant. "Particularly since I've a reputation which should compel any mother worthy of the name to keep her daughters clear of me. I also have a fortune, however, and some considerable expectations—do I not offend my conniving grandmama."

She frowned a little at this vulgarity. "I see. But your grandmama must be very fond of you, surely, else she'd not go to so much trouble."

"It is trouble wasted! I've not the remotest intention of attending their revolting Matrimonial Stakes Ball!"

"Oh, but you must! If it is given in your honour you could not refuse to attend. That would be so unkind."

"Another facet of my character. You are learning fast, ma'am."

"Yes." Her eyes sparkled at him. "And I rate your unkindness quite on a par with your—tidiness, Mr. Savage."

He was hurt, which was ridiculous, but before he could voice some of the bitter remarks that rose to his tongue, a laugh trilled out from the hall and Mrs. Netty, fully dressed and with an apron tied round her small middle, came to join them. "How very droll you look, Mr. Savage. If you are not the kindest gentleman to make my dear Miss Primrose laugh so."

To make Mrs. Hythe laugh had not been Savage's aim at that particular instant, but a swift glance at the widow showed him a merry face, and she said in a distinctly amused voice, "Not really droll, but I think you had best look to your—tidiness, sir."

With Mrs. Netty's giggles ringing in his ears, he hurried to the mirror that hung in the withdrawing room. His appearance caused him to recoil in horror. When he'd searched for Consuela, convinced that she was hiding, he'd been very thorough, peering under beds, moving aside the garments that hung in presses, and being impeded by long coats and gowns as he poked about. At one point a hat box had fallen and the bonnets it contained had showered down on him. He'd fought his way out of the things, but it was now obvious that to an extent he'd brought one of them with him. His hair was wildly disordered, with curls sticking up all over his head. And among them was a demure pink velvet bow.

Wrenching the bow from his hair, he snarled, "Oh, my God!" and beat a fast retreat to his bedchamber. Lord, but he was a sight! The widow's dimple was explained now. He'd been braying about tidiness while looking like an unmade bed. In the act of dragging the hairbrush through his disordered locks, his hand was arrested. The Spotted Hythe had said, with her long eyes full of mischief, that she rated his unkindness on a par with his tidiness. And considering his appearance at that moment...

A weight seemed to lift from his spirits. He'd been so busy that there had been little time to devote to the more pleasurable aspects of his stay here. But now Miss Underhill would come every day, and Mrs. Netty was up and about. Pay was here also, which was unfortunate, but now that he'd rested his eyes on the plump prettiness of the vicar's daughter, he would be fully occupied. Besides which, he'd be starting back to Town very soon. Meanwhile, it would do no harm to change clothes and present a better face to the widow. Then, he would set forth to find the child. Paynton would never be able to do so, for although he was a good enough man, the cargo he carried between his ears had capsized long since.

Savage paused, vexed with himself, as he arranged a clean neckcloth. Years ago, someone had made that unkind observation. Who in the deuce was it? Oh, yes. Furness. It had annoyed him at the time, and although Pay had merely shrugged and paid no heed, he'd blacked Furness's eye because of it. Of course, he'd been feeling more charitable towards Paynton then.

His thoughts drifted back to the widow. She would be pleased when he found her child. She really was quite a pretty creature, which he'd have realized at once had it not been for cobwebs and spots. She'd made it perfectly clear that she had no desire to find herself another husband, which was another point in her favour. And since she no longer appeared to be as afraid of him as when he'd first arrived, it might be rather amusing to enter into a small dalliance with the lady.

He began to whistle merrily as he arranged a ruby pin in his neckcloth.

He was not then, of course, aware of the complications of Milor' and the exotic fowl.

CHAPTER FIVE

WHEN SAVAGE STROLLED DOWN the stairs some ten minutes later, except for his scratches, he managed to present a picture of elegance, his dark curls brushed into an attractively tumbled style, his claret coloured long tailed coat adhering to his broad shoulders with only a slight wrinkle (which would have caused his man to wail with horror), breeches clinging to muscular thighs, and top boots gleaming (thanks to the strong application of a towel—which would probably have reduced his man to tears).

His pleasant smile became a scowl however, when he went into the withdrawing room. Paynton and Miss Underhill had returned, and Consuela sat on her mother's lap, weeping heartbrokenly.

"There you are, Leo," remarked Paynton, with a sad want of originality. "All ready to leave, eh?"

"I merely changed my dress for luncheon," said Savage, waiting for the widow to notice him.

"And very nice you do look," remarked Mrs. Netty, bustling in. "Now, Miss Consuela, you must not upset yourself so. I'm sure Milor' will come home."

The child lifted a tear-streaked face and pointed a chubby finger at Savage. "Him fright Milor' 'way! Him too rough wiv soap!"

"Well, if that don't beat the Dutch," protested the accused. "Only look at what I suffered because you said it was easy to give the br—to bathe the animal."

"That is quite true, dear," said Mrs. Hythe gently. "Mr. Savage was only trying to help, and you must not now blame him because Milor' has wandered off."

"Milor' fright 'way," sobbed Consuela, tearful eyes unrelenting.

"I wouldn't think Mr. Savage *meant* to frighten the poor little fella," said Paynton. "He don't know much about cats, is what it _is_."

Savage slanted a glance at him that might well have blistered his skin, and said that he was too kind. Crossing to drop to one knee beside the widow, he said in his kindest voice, "Tell you what, little one. After lunch you and I will go out and find Milor'."

Mrs. Hythe gave him a grateful smile.

"Capital notion," said Paynton heartily.

"After you leave," said Savage with a grim stare.

"No, no. I'll wait for you, dear boy. Promised your sire, y'know."

"Her finded him," Consuela said with tragic disappointment as she shrank from Savage's outstretched hand. "Why him chase Milor' 'way?"

Much to Savage's relief, Miss Underhill came in and took the little girl off to be washed and fed her lunch.

Mrs. Hythe said, "I must apologize for my daughter, Mr. Savage. I only hope the cat has not come to harm. He is most affectionate and never wanders away for more than an hour or so."

"Been gone a lot longer than that, ma'am," said Paynton, with exactitude if not tact. "If he's fallen into some drift and froze, we ain't likely to find him 'til the thaw."

The distress in the widow's face disturbed Savage. "What fustian you do talk, Pay," he exclaimed. "I fancy the brute is merely stalking a pigeon or he may have developed a taste for duck. I never saw a cat with such an appetite."

"Well, in case you don't find him," said Paynton, "I'll fetch the little gal a new pet, or a toy of some kind. Take her mind off things, y'know."

The widow smiled from Paynton's sympathetic face to Savage's glowering one. "You both are most kind. Even so, we cannot detain you any longer, Mr. Savage. You've a special reason now for returning to Town."

"And a more compelling reason for *not* returning," he murmured.

"Luncheon is served, Miss Primrose," said Mrs. Netty.

"Miss Underhill and I will make our own search after luncheon, so you may be *à l'aise,*" said Paynton, patting Mrs. Hythe's hand as he assisted her to her feet.

"I'll bundle Consuela up warm and close, ma'am." Savage elbowed Paynton aside and offered the widow his arm. "We'll find the cat, I promise you."

Mrs. Netty announced her intention of putting hot compresses on the widow's ankle, and although Mrs. Hythe protested that her foot was almost better, she was borne off relentlessly as soon as luncheon was finished.

Paynton winked at Savage conspiratorially and said he would go up and look in on "Poor Elstow." Since Miss Underhill had already gone upstairs to read to the invalid, Savage's suspicions were allayed. Miss Underhill was a little on the plump side, but rather delightfully so, and there was a gleam in her blue eyes that was not strange to him. The vicar's daughter was aware that she was a pretty creature and was not above a little flirting. 'Not two brains to rub together, but just the type Pay likes,' he thought, and went off with Consuela to resume the search.

An hour later, having again scoured the enormous barn and various outbuildings, they decided to try the abbey. On the way, Savage's keen eyes detected a clump of black fur and some tracks which

looked so ominously like those of a fox, that he diverted the child's attention and scraped the snow
over them quickly. Milor' was a monster with the
appetite of two monsters, and could undoubtedly
take care of any pigeon, or duck, that came within
his range. However, if the cat had been attacked
from behind by a fox, it was all too probable that he
had met his fate. Savage tried to prepare the child by
telling her that Milor' might very well have become
bored with the snow, and headed for Cornwall or
Devonshire, "where palm trees grow and it never
snows." She heard him out in silence, but it was evi-
dent that his remarks had not convinced her.

It was very cold, with an icy wind blowing, and he
suggested they should return to the warm house.
Consuela eyed him with grievous disappointment,
and raised her arms. "Up."

He lifted her, glad that she no longer shrank from
him, and surprised to discover how necessary to his
peace of mind she had become.

She patted his cheek, and said with sad resigna-
tion, "Her finded him."

The great sigh that followed made him desperate
to redeem himself. Abandoning his hope for a warm
fireside and a cose with the widow, he promised,
"And he will not give up 'til we have looked everywhere."

His reward was a hug that came near to strangling him, and a smacking kiss that stripped more armour from his already somewhat besieged heart.

He carried her all the way up the hill, making her laugh a little with his puffing and groaning. And he thought that if the cat had indeed perished, he would ride at once into the village and buy her a dog—any kind of dog. A St. Bernard, preferably. Anything to take the grief from her innocent eyes.

When they entered the frowning gloom of the ruins, he remembered the widow's warnings and insisted that Consuela stay close beside him.

"Course," she said, and a moment later darted away and disappeared.

His wrathful shouts were ignored, and he suffered some unpleasant moments as he sought about until a door creaked open behind him, and Consuela reappeared. The tears that streaked her cheeks extinguished the anger that had been building in him. "Where the deuce have you been?" he demanded without much force.

She gestured to the blackness beyond the door. "Her look in a' cellars."

Savage peered down stone steps into stygian gloom. Awed, he muttered, "Good God! You went down there?"

"Her knows how," she said, drying her eyes on his cuff. "Milor' not there. He would've comed when her called. Milor' runned 'way."

"Well, don't cry, little one," he said bracingly.
"Let's keep on looking."

And so they wandered from one dismal and cobwebby chamber, to another. Savage kept tight hold
of the child's hand now, and would not permit that
they go upstairs, but he joined her in calling for
Milor', and, having been instructed that his roar
would merely frighten the cat farther away, he
meekly adjusted his tones to the high-pitched squeak
she felt suitable. That did make her laugh, and it was
with an improved relationship that they went into the
next room.

It was a vast, cold, and forbidding chamber, with
empty bookcases proclaiming it to have once been
the library. Not until they were inside did Savage realize that this was the room Mrs. Hythe had so ve-
hemently refused to enter. He felt a strong sense of
guilt, and started to turn back, although the place
was quite empty, and if there was anything in here
that could hold the least interest for him, he wished
he might see it.

And then he saw the painting.

Almost life-size, it hung above the great hearth in
forlorn state. Curious, he walked closer, while Consuela trotted about opening cupboard doors and
calling piercingly for her pet. Savage gazed up at the
portrait of two little girls, and marvelled that the
widow, who so patently adored her daughter, should
allow this splendid work to be abandoned. The art-

ist had imparted a slightly more mature look to
Consuela, but the likeness was excellent, and he had
captured to admiration both her childish loveliness
and the aura of mischief that hung about her. Savage turned his attention to the second girl. She appeared a year or so younger, little more than a tot,
with a sweetly rounded face and soft brown curls,
and she clung to Consuela's skirts, gazing at her with
a touchingly fond expression.

Roused by a tug at his breeches, Savage said,
"This is a beautiful painting, Consuela. Why ever is
it not in the house?"

"Milor' not here," she said single-mindedly.

"I'm sorry. We'll try the next room. Er—who is
the other little girl?"

The big blue eyes were raised to the portrait.
"Mama."

Savage smiled. "No, no. This is a picture of you,
dear. I meant—"

The small head swathed in its scarf was shaken
vigorously. "Mama," she repeated. "An' Aunty
Kathy."

Stunned, he returned his gaze to the painting. Mrs.
Hythe was, he had come to realize, a quite lovely
young woman, but the golden ringlets of the older
child had surely not been hers? He pointed to the
smaller girl. "This is your Aunty Kathy?"

"No. Mama." A great sigh was gathered. "Aunt
Kathy 'n angel."

"What a pity," he said. "Jove, but you look like her."

Slow tears gathered and to his horror, overflowed again. "P'raps," she gulped, "Milor' goed a' find her."

THE HOUSE WAS WARM and welcoming after the bleak out-of-doors, and although it was only half-past three, candlelight glowed from the withdrawing room windows. Stamping the snow from his boots, Savage released the unhappy Consuela to the care of a tenderly sympathetic Mrs. Netty and shrugged out of his coat and hat. Shivering, he went in search of the widow, and found her seated on the sofa before the withdrawing room fire, engrossed in knitting a scarf.

He paused, looking at her. The light of the flames awoke golden gleams from the luxuriant curls that clustered about her ears. She wore a woollen gown of soft rose pink, cut low at the throat and edged with a little Betsy ruff. Her cap, which was charming, vexed him, for he judged it a deliberate attempt to make her look matronly, which was ridiculous since she could not possibly be much more than three and twenty, but it was the only thing to spoil what could only be judged an enchanting picture. He watched the skilled and graceful movements of her hands. The scarf was already quite a length, stripes of white and claret alternating with wider stripes of light blue.

It looked, he thought, like a man's scarf, and would be soft and warm in weather such as this. He frowned at it, wondering how many admirers clustered around the widow.

As if she sensed his regard her head swung up suddenly and she exclaimed, "Oh, you are back! Pray come and warm your hands, Mr. Savage, you look frozen. Did you—er...?"

He hurried to the fire and followed her advice, saying quietly, "I am rather inclined to think a fox dealt Milor' his quietus, ma'am."

She said nothing.

Turning his head to glance at her, he gave a gasp. One hand was pressed to her mouth. Over it, her eyes, wide and stricken, blinked at him tearfully.

Scarcely conscious of moving, he was beside her on the sofa, and had gathered her into his arms. "No, never grieve so, brave little lady," he said, his voice a husky caress. "Jove, but I'm a clumsy dolt!"

"Yes," she sobbed into his neckcloth. "But the p-poor little...cat!"

"Tears—from you?" He smiled tenderly. "Such a soft heart, for all your courage in having faced the world alone all these years."

She drew back, wiping at her eyes ineffectually. "It's j-just that... We have all become so—so fond of the dear creature."

"Of course you have." With the expertise of long practice, he dabbed his handkerchief at her tears.

"But pray do not weep, Mrs. Primrose. I doubt the cat suffered, and I shall find you another. I promise."

"You are very kind." She appropriated his handkerchief and blew her nose daintily.

He had seldom known a lady resort to so prosaic an action before him, and he chuckled.

"However, I think Sir Everard went in search of one," she added.

Savage's smile vanished. "Went in search of—what, pray?"

"Another cat for Consuela." She smiled at him tremulously. "Is it not kind that he would go out in such dreadful weather for the sake of a little child?"

He refrained from pointing out that he had just tramped through miles of snow and freezing draughty old buldings for the sake of a little child, and said a somewhat dour, "Hum," then added, "I suppose so, for he is not her papa, after all." He felt the widow stiffen, but he went on as if in an afterthought, "I have meant to ask where is his picture, ma'am?"

"Do you not mean, Spotted Hythe, sir?"

She spoke in a teasing way, but she was pale suddenly, and he knew she was attempting to turn his thoughts. "That I was ever so cruel as to make such a gauche remark," he sighed. "I can but throw myself on your mercy, ma'am, and most humbly beg your pardon."

She touched his arm with rather sweet shyness. "All gentlemen are cruel at times. But very few are so kind as you, a complete stranger, have been to us."

"Thank you, but surely you must not have found Consuela's father to be a cruel gentleman?"

Her hand was withdrawn. In a colourless voice she said, "He was the kindest of men, and completely devoted to me."

"Perfectly understandable. What gentleman would not revere so lovely a wife. How he must have adored Consuela."

"He died while—while she was still in the cradle."

"Great heavens! I recall you had said he passed away while you travelled—in Italy, I think? How frightful for you, ma'am! Had you help available? I fancy his family must have rushed to offer their aid."

His sympathetic interest seemed to heighten her nervousness. "He was a younger son," she said slowly, "and was cut off when he chose to study art in Rome rather than follow a military career, as his father desired."

"And so you were abandoned? If ever I heard of such a thing! I wonder you did not starve. Oh—but you had your own family, of course."

"Yes." She smiled fondly. "Papa and my mother were more than kind."

"They approved of Mr. Hythe, then? Despite his lack of expectations?"

Her eyes fell. "He had very great talent," she said evasively. "We all expected him to become famous. And—and everyone liked Ambrose."

"He must have been a remarkable man. May I see his picture?"

Her eyes were still downcast. She said, "Alas, I do not have one, sir. Would that I did."

"Jove! Not even a miniature, or a sketch?"

"No." She looked up then, her eyes cold with suspicion. "May I ask what has awoken this sudden interest, Mr. Savage?"

He shrugged, and said disarmingly, "I'll own my heart has been won, ma'am."

At once she looked frightened again. She all but cringed from him! "By your beautiful daughter," he added. Her relief was so palpable that he could have shaken her. "I wondered," he said through his teeth, "if she resembled her papa. In which case he must have been a fine-looking fellow."

"I think you imply that Consuela does not favour me." She gave a nervous little laugh. "La, sir, I know I am no beauty, but it is unkind in you to remark it."

"Such was not my intent, for I find you very lovely indeed. But in a rather different style, so I thought—"

"And quite rightly, sir. Consuela does indeed favour her father. Ambrose was very fair and exceeding handsome."

"Ah. That is how it must be, then. I had fancied
perhaps she took after some uncle or aunt, perhaps."

"No. My brother was dark and my only sister
was—was very like me." She took up her scarf again.
"They used in fact to take us for twins."

Twins? He frowned. "You would seem to have
suffered rather more than your share of tragedy,
ma'am. I've a sister of my own who is very dear to
me, so I can comprehend that to lose both her and
your husband within so short a period must have
been very hard."

She was knitting at a great rate of speed, although
it seemed to him that the needles clashed much more
than they had done before, and that her movements
were jerky and erratic. They stopped abruptly. Her
eyes flew to his face. "Had I told you about Katherine, then? Dear me, I had not meant to lay all my
troubles in your dish, sir."

He responded impulsively, "It would be my
delight to relieve you of 'em, ma'am."

The rosy colour surged back into her face, and the
fear in her eyes was banished by a very different
emotion. Suddenly, his heart was pounding at an
unprecedented rate. Her busy hands stilled, and he

covered them with one of his own. "Primrose..." he whispered, and leaned to her.

"Is anyone about?" Paynton's jovial tones rang through the hushed silence. "Only see what I have found! *Consuela?* Where are you, little miss?"

Jerked rudely from that enchanted moment, Savage stood hurriedly and strolled to the door, yearning for a war axe.

Paynton, the scarf still wrapped round his throat, and with his cheeks aglow, was coming into the kitchen, carrying a large wooden box.

Squeaking with excitement, Consuela tumbled down the stairs, Miss Underhill hurrying after her. Surprised, for he had assumed the vicar's daughter to have gone with Paynton, Savage drawled, "It cannot be a new pony, certainly."

Consuela giggled, flew to seize Paynton by the leg and hug it, then cried an impatient, "Open! Open!"

"One moment," said Savage, and returned to usher the widow into the room. Strange noises were coming from inside the box. Consuela began to jump up and down as with a great air of mystery Paynton lowered it to the floor. Mrs. Netty screamed a request that they wait until she came, and then Consuela's eyes grew very round and she said solemnly, "Ev' one but Brettoe."

"Well, we can't have that," said Savage, sweeping the widow without ceremony into his arms.

"What on earth—" she gasped.

"Everybody upstairs," decreed Savage, happily aware of the soft arm that had slid round his neck.

The procession wound up the stairs to the room of an invalid who looked at them with a dreamy smile that sent Savage's eyes to the blushing cheeks of the vicar's daughter.

"Now," said Savage, settling the widow on the solitary chair, "we are all together. Unveil your find, Sir Everard."

Paynton, rather out of breath, put his crate on the end of the bed and began to take off the ill-fitting lid.

"Wazzit? Wazzit?"

Squeaking with excitement, Consuela scrambled onto the bed and pulled impatiently at the top of the box at the same moment that Elstow, who was beginning to look less wan, hoisted himself onto an elbow. The box tilted. There was a great deal of consternation, and two small creatures rushed forth and began to dash about at great speed, squawking and fluttering frenziedly.

"What the—deuce . . . ?" gasped Savage.

Elstow began to make muffled wheezing noises.

"Good—gracious me . . ." said the widow, her dimple provoked.

"If those are—cats," said Savage, putting up his quizzing glass and surveying the frantic creatures, "I'll eat 'em!"

Consuela wailed, "Him *not* eat! Sir Everdid finded them for *her!*"

"'Course I did, m'dear," said Paynton, indignant. "Wasn't what I started out for, mind. But—better'n nought, eh, Mrs. Primrose?"

"They're—lovely," said the widow, a trifle unsteadily.

"And—what*ever* they are—would be better off my bed," wheezed Elstow.

Savage captured one of the new pets and over its shrill outcries said, "*Whatever* they are, indeed!"

"They her fluffy chicky's," said Consuela, beaming at Sir Everard.

"And the most undersized—" began Savage.

"No, but they're so pretty," intervened the widow, holding her face away from a pair of wildly beating wings as she restored the second "pet" to its box. "And—and rare. I never in all my life saw—er, chickens like this."

"Nor did anyone else, I'll warrant," said Savage. "Where the devil did you find 'em, Pay?"

"In the village, dear boy. Some old duck at the inn had bought 'em off a foreign schooner at Portsmouth, but the host's wife wouldn't have 'em on the property. Said they was—" he glanced at Consuela, and spelled out, "B-e-w-i-t-c-h-e-d, and e-v-i-l. I thought the little gal might have more sense."

"They wouldn't make a chicken s-a-n-d-w-i-c-h between 'em," snorted Savage.

"Well, they—they might be good layers," offered the widow, with determined optimism.

"If you like to eat marbles," grunted Savage, noticing how delightfully her eyes sparkled when she was amused.

"Them got feathery feet," said Consuela, peering into the crate rapturously. "Her love them." Her little face turned up to him trustingly. "Where them go to bed, Mr. Leo?"

"In the henhouse, of course," said Elstow.

"No! It too cold," Consuela protested.

Sir Everard nodded. "Got a point. 'Sides, the regular sort of brutes might—er, take exception to 'em. Better build 'em a separate little house, old fellow."

Savage stared at him. "One can but hope you speak in jest."

"Well, I don't. I'll remind you that *I* found 'em. The least *you* can do is to provide a shelter for 'em."

The widow said demurely, "Thank you, Sir Everard. You are all kindness. But we must not keep imposing on poor Mr. Savage. Besides, he likely does not have the faintest notion of how to build a henhouse. Perhaps Miss Faith and I can manage to—"

"Madam," snarled Savage. "You would not believe the henhouses I have built!"

She twinkled at him. "They doubtless litter your home in Town, eh, sir?"

"The back lawns are fairly cluttered with 'em! All shapes and sizes."

"They are?" said Sir Everard, astonished. "I never saw—"

"Then you shall see one tomorrow," said Savage. "For as soon as I return from the village, my enterprising procurer of exotic fowl, you shall help me construct a regular palace of a henhouse!"

CHAPTER SIX

WHEN SAVAGE SET OUT early next morning, bright sunlight striking the white-carpeted world dazzled his eyes. The air was still cold enough to turn breath into small clouds, but by the time he reached the track leading to Dingly Down little clumps of snow were dropping from the trees. He guided the horse carefully, keeping to patches of the lane that were not frozen solid. A wain lumbered towards him, and the cheerful driver imparted the news that the turnpike must be fairly clear because he'd seen a stagecoach that had got through from Godalming. Deciding to verify this, Savage passed the village track and rode on until he reached the turnpike. Traffic was light, but traffic there was, both vehicles and riders. If the weather held, he and Paynton could likely reach Town by afternoon. He smiled faintly, knowing he had no least intention of depriving The Spotted Hythe of her new paying guest. The brisk air had sharpened his appetite however, and before turning back, he rode into the yard of The Merry Monk, a fine posting house he often patronized on his way down to Whitecaps.

His arrival created quite a stir, the host, Elijah
Stubbs, coming out to greet him, and the pretty
serving maids all smiles and curtsies for the famous
Corinthian. He was relieved of his riding coat, hat,
scarf, and gloves, and shown to a table in the tap,
close to the roaring fire. A fragrantly steaming glass
of mulled wine was brought to him. Mine host per-
sonally carried over a platter of succulent ham, assorted cheeses, and bread and muffins still warm
from the oven. Applying himself to this pleasing
fare, Savage felt the cold seep from his bones and
began to be comfortably warm and quite in charity
with his fellow man and the world in general.

"As I live and breathe, it's The Savage!"

Only eight words, but the nasal drawl brought a
grin to Savage's lips, and he stood, holding out his
hand. "What brings you into the country, Furness?
A wench? Or a parcel of 'em?"

"You misjudge me, dear boy." Sir Conrad Furness pulled out a chair and sat down, uninvited. He
still wore his long driving coat, the capes emphasiz-
ing a pair of powerful shoulders, and a high crowned
beaver hat was set at a rakish angle on his dark hair.
The smile that curved his mouth was friendly, but the
rather hard dark eyes were veiled. "Moreover,"
Furness went on, "It appears I might better ask that
question of you." He tapped his riding whip gently
against Savage's scratched face. "A reluctant chit, I
apprehend."

Savage chuckled. "An extreme reluctant wildcat. Dead now, poor creature," he added.

Furness's bland smile was banished and his jaw sagged. *"Dead?"* he gasped. "Do you say…you…" He laughed, recovering himself. "I'd believe a lot of you, rogue, but not murder of a female, I think."

"No? I'll own I've come close to it these past few days."

Stretching out his long legs, Furness waved to the host and helped himself to a muffin. "Do I detect an amorous escapade? I had it on the—er, best authority that you left Town in a rush and were bound for your grandmama's home in Portsmouth."

The host came up with a tankard of ale, and a promise to let Sir Conrad know when his team was ready. Furness nodded to him, then raised his tankard to Savage and said with a chuckle, "What happened? Trapped by the snow, I'll wager. Stuck in this bucolic desolation, and not a fair Paphian in sight. Poor fellow, what a ghastly fate!"

"To the contrary, I have been vastly diverted. In fact," added Savage musingly, "I've routed boredom for nigh a week. Something of a record."

As he watched Savage, Sir Conrad's smile was replaced by a thoughtful expression. "Come now, Leo," he coaxed. "I've had the deuce of a drive and must push on to Town, for I'm already late for a meeting with my damned man of business. Take pity on a weary traveller and cheer my oppressed spirits

with a tale of conquest. Who is it, dear boy? If
you've been marooned nearby I fancy you've had
your pick of the damsels in More-or-Less and Dingly
Down. Egad! What a rare selection! Unless..." He
pursed his lips. "Can it be that you've stumbled onto
the delectable widow?"

Savage tensed, and turned his head to surprise an
oddly intent look on the baronet's features. "The
delectable widow?" drawled Savage. "Jupiter! Have
I missed something?"

Sir Conrad laughed and leaned back in his chair
again. "Nothing worth having, I promise you."

For just an instant Savage sat very still. Then he
said cynically, "Not if *you've* more than a speaking
acquaintanceship with the lady, certainly."

"Oho, what a setdown! And whatever else, the
word 'lady' don't belong in this conversation. A fair
piece, but," Furness winked suggestively, "one that
might better be called love's lady lost."

Savage lifted his brows. "A trollop?"

"How very ungentlemanly of me did I confirm
that," said Furness, grinning broadly.

"Very true. But I really feel you should either fish
or cut line."

Something in Savage's tone sent Sir Conrad's
narrowed glance darting to search the younger man's
face. Finding it expressionless, he said heartily, "My
dear fellow—if you've an interest there, I'll be mum!

From what you said, I'd thought you had not met the wild widow."

"Wild, is it? Gad, Furness, but you begin to interest me. Does she run a gaming house in the barn? Or is your widow a female rank rider, perhaps?"

"Less flamboyant than that, I promise you." Furness leaned closer and lowered his voice. "She has a child, yet I am told would be—" he chuckled "—devilish hard put to it to produce her marriage lines!"

The host came bustling up. "Your pardon, gentlemen. Sir Conrad, your carriage is at the door. Best not keep your horses standing in this cold."

"Right you are, by Jove!" Furness stood, and with a hurried exhortation that Savage "'Ware all widows," he was gone, shouting a farewell over his shoulder.

Savage, who had come to his feet, caught Mr. Stubbs's eye and sat down again.

"More wine, sir?"

"To the devil with your wine, Stubbs!"

The host shrugged apologetically. "Happens I recollect the last time I see that look on your face, Mr. Savage. You and the gentleman fought upstairs, and there was I, trying to tell the customers 'twas a dancing party—till he was carried down." Mr. Stubbs shook his head gravely. "Things like that give a house a bad name."

"Fiddle! Add a bit of spice, more like. Besides, you're quite mistaken. If I looked irked—it was over an—er, another matter." Savage's lips tightened again, then he smiled. "You old fool—I'd fancied you knew by now that Sir Conrad Furness is my friend."

"I'd thought that sir, to be sure. Certain it is that I'd be sorry to ever see the two of you come to cuffs." He grinned suddenly. "And sorrier to miss it!"

"Damn you! Do you want me dead? We're too closely matched by far!" The host looked troubled, and Savage laughed at him. "Don't be so glum, man! I know you mean well. I'll have my reckoning now, and be on my way. I've work to do!"

It was, as Mr. Stubbs told his life's companion a short while later, enough to make a honest man come over queer-like, to hear a gentleman of the Quality speak of himself and work in the same breath!

"What a silly you are, Stubbs," said his lady merrily. "Mr. Savage likely means to sit down and paint a picture—that's the kind of thing he would think of as work!"

The good lady would have been considerably surprised had she looked into the large barn at Erskine Abbey later that afternoon. Clad in an old greatcoat which had belonged to the late Mr. John Erskine, and looking very much the captain of his crew, Leopold Savage was superintending two villagers in the unloading of a waggon that had arrived from Dingly Down. "Put that barrel of nails over there," he said briskly. "And keep the planks separated according to length."

"Good gracious," exclaimed Mrs. Hythe, who formed one of the small crowd watching the procedure. "I did not dream it would take so much wood—"

"Lumber, ma'am," corrected Savage knowledgeably.

"Mean to build to last do you, Leo?" enquired Paynton innocently.

"I do not hold with half measures, if that's what you mean. You and I will erect a henhouse Mrs. Hythe may be proud of. Unless, of course, you feel the task is beyond you?"

"No such thing," asserted Paynton, aware that a certain pair of pretty eyes were fixed admiringly upon him. "My very great pleasure to be of assistance to the lady. So long as we get back to Town within a day or two. Promised your father, y'know."

"No problem there, my tulip. We'll have it done and the tenants installed by this time tomorrow!"

Two days later, Sir Everard straightened his aching back and laid aside the saw. "When you said we would build a palace of a henhouse, Leo," he grumbled, "I'd not realized you meant it literally!"

Hammering lustily, Savage said, "Stuff! We're doing marvellously. Did ever you see a better house?"

Paynton surveyed the results of their labours with a sceptical eye. "Never saw one like it, at all events. Is it supposed to get narrow like that at the back end?"

"It ain't your old fashioned uninspired henhouse, if that's what you mean." Peering towards the rear of the structure, Savage held the next nail steady. "One puts something of oneself into such endeavours, and— Hell and damnation!" He dropped the hammer and commenced an energetic dance round the barn, nursing his left hand, and swearing as he went.

"Good thing you came in, ma'am," said Paynton, grinning unfeelingly. "Leo put something of himself into the henhouse. A bit of thumb, I think."

Mrs. Hythe gave a cry of sympathy and flew to take Savage's wounded hand and demand to be allowed to see.

Holding his breath and choking back profanities, he followed her to the area at the side of the stove which had become their temporary dispensary. He sat down on the barrel as instructed, and began to feel less victimized as the widow bathed and anointed his hurt, tied the bandage, and patted his hand with tender solicitude. "Poor soul," she murmured. "And you were doing so well."

He sighed. "The nail bent on a knot, ma'am, else I'd never have missed my stroke."

"Such a nasty place." She watched interestedly as he stroked her fingers. "It must pain you terribly. You cannot work without your thumb, sir. Perhaps we should send for the carpenter at More-or—"

"Certainly not! I promised Consuela I would build a house for her pets. Besides, it is almost done, as you can plainly see."

"Er—yes," said the widow, peering.

Savage saw a furtive dimple. "You don't like it," he accused.

"But I do, indeed!"

"Oh, dear!" exclaimed Miss Underhill, hurrying to join them. "Not another accident?"

"Nothing to matter, ma'am," declared Paynton nobly.

Mrs. Hythe said, "Mr. Savage thinks I do not like his house, Faith."

Her eyes, turned from Savage, were sparkling with laughter, but with a commendable effort Miss Underhill managed to keep her own face grave. "How could we fail to like it, sir?" she said. "When it is truly so remarkable."

"Ain't the word I'd have used," muttered Paynton.

"I agree," said the widow, and as Savage turned her chin to look suspiciously into her eyes, she added guilelessly, "*Unique* is a better term. The back porch, especially."

Routed by her saintly expression, he could barely suppress an urge to smile. "Wretched widow! It is nothing of the kind, and you know it."

She gave a muffled gurgle of mirth. Enchanted by those vivid lips, he bent lower, murmuring, "You should be—"

Consuela's shriek made two people jump, and disappointed two onlookers. "Oooh! Her henhouse is *boo*tiful!" Dancing round it, she asked, "Is him going to put the roof on afore he puts in the perches?"

"Perches?" Savage rubbed his chin. "Oh, Egad!" He glanced at his friend.

"A home question," sighed Sir Everard. "I wonder why I've the feeling I am to be despatched to Dingly Down."

"Well, if you are, sir," said Miss Underhill demurely, "I wonder if I might go with you? I want to fetch my party dress so that I may change here."

"With the greatest pleasure in the world," declared Sir Everard, brightening. "Is there to be a party, Mrs. Primrose?"

"Tomorrow afternoon," she answered, "we are going to celebrate the completion of the henhouse, and the fact that Barrett is allowed to get up."

"An' we're to have a *cake!*" chortled Consuela. "An' Mama will play her pinafore an' sing for us!"

Preserving his countenance admirably, Savage said, ''We must work like Trojans, Pay, so as to be done in time, for on no account will I miss hearing Mrs. Primrose play her pinafore!''

The widow's musical trill of laughter rippled out.

He turned to watch her, and her mirth faded into uncertainty as she encountered a bleak look she had all but forgotten. It vanished as suddenly as it had appeared, and he was saying lightly, ''Do you saddle up, Pay, whilst I take the measurements for the perches.''

Despite his throbbing hand, he laboured steadily after Sir Everard and Miss Underhill had driven out in his now repaired curricle. His task was hindered by his disabled thumb, and he hammered more cautiously. Whatever would his father and Grandmama think if they could see him at this moment? Or if they knew what he was— A delicate fragrance was on the air. He swung about eagerly.

''It is only The Spotted Hythe,'' said the widow.

He glanced at the bowl she carried.

''We finished icing the cake,'' she explained. ''I supposed that like all little boys you might like to clean it out.''

He took the bowl and set it on the diminished pile of lumber. ''But you see, I am not a little boy,'' he pointed out, taking her hands. ''And I have you all to myself, at last!''

"That will teach me to make a kindly gesture."
She shook her head at him, and as he drew her closer,
she pushed against his chest. "No, Leo. I brought
you the icing—only."

"Your lips are sweeter than any icing ever con-
cocted in this world," he murmured, kissing her
temple although she averted her face. "And you
make it devilish hard, Unspotted Hythe, to—" And
suddenly Conrad Furness's laughing voice was in his
ears again— "She has a child, yet I am told would be
devilish hard put to it to produce her marriage
lines..." He stood very still. The widow's check-
ered past should be an added inducement, rather
than repelling him, for she could never be more than
a pleasant dalliance, after all.

Mrs. Hythe looked up at him curiously. The pale
winter sunlight slanted through the door, painting a
faint sheen upon the delicate curve of her cheek and
awakening the amber flecks in her eyes. He had never
really appreciated the dainty line of her nose, and
below them that lovely mouth was—

And she had not so much as a sketch of her late
husband...

He said with his easy smile, "But I must remember to be a gentleman, especially when there is no one
here to defend you against my wicked advances. To
console myself, I shall attend to this bowl you have
generously brought me. And further, ma'am, from
this day forth, the barn is out of bounds to all but

Paynton and myself. We mean the finished article to
be a real surprise.''

The widow glanced at the half-finished article.
''Oh—I am sure it will be,'' said she, with the mer-
est flicker of a dimple.

''I SAY, SIR,'' said Elston, surveying Savage's elegance admiringly. ''You look complete to a shade.
It's jolly good of you to come and give me a hand.''

Holding the invalid's shirt while he shrugged into
it, Savage said, ''This is an event. Not only are you
recovered, but you are to view the results of what Pay
and I have laboured on these long weary days.''

Elstow grinned and applied himself to buttons.
''Such a trial we have been to you, when you did but
mean to overnight. I cannot apologize enough.''

''Do not dare. I've enjoyed myself more than—''
He broke off, and busied himself selecting a coat
from the young man's meagre wardrobe. ''There. I
think the fawn will do the business; the claret would
make you look wan.''

''Really, you are too good, sir.''

''You may think me far from good when you see
our henhouse. It is very sturdy, mind, but just a trifle—er, unorthodox, perhaps. Here are your shoes.
Good God! A terrible thought occurs to me! Are you
by any chance a gifted carpenter?''

Sitting on the bed, Elstow said ruefully, "I'm not gifted at anything much, alas. Why should that be a terrible thought?"

"I recollected your interest in architecture, and feared that might perhaps indicate a flair for building things. Well, I'm relieved that you won't be holding my efforts up to scorn."

"Gad, sir," said Elstow indignantly. "As if I would be so ungrateful!"

"I rejoice to hear it. I'd a feeling The Spotted Hythe—I mean, your cousin Primrose, looked at the henhouse with just a trace of, er—criticism. Now for the neckcloth. Lift your chin and sit very still. Ah, but I'll wager I know what is my problem! The late Mr. Hythe was likely skilled in such matters, was he?"

"I've no idea, sir." With his head tilted upward, Elstow did not see how narrowly Savage watched him, and he went on innocently, "Prim married Hythe in Italy, you see. And he died before they returned to England, poor fellow. I believe his family hailed from Saffron Walden—or was it Colchester? Somewhere out that way. Prim said he was a most talented artist, but I never heard her mention that he built anything in the carpentry line. I'd fancy his health would have kept him from any sort of strenuous effort."

"Then I'm reprieved, thank heaven! Up with you, my lad, and see what I've wrought."

Elstow stood and, surveying himself in the mirror, murmured, "Oh, Jupiter! I never looked so fine. I wonder if she will—" He broke off, his pale face reddening. "That is to say—I mean—"

"I know just what you mean, you young rogue. And she's a lovely little lady. I'd think you would deal very well together. Have you approached the vicar in the matter?"

"No, sir." Elstow hesitated, then said shyly, "In fact—I would be most grateful of your advice. I've very little to offer her as yet, but Faith is willing to wait, and if I could just get a position with an architect… Do you think I should declare myself now, or say nothing until I'm better situated? I'd—I'd not impose on you sir, but you've been so very good to us, and you know your way about the world."

Savage's eyes fell. If the poor lad knew how he had just been used! He said in a rather strained voice, "In my experience, Barrett, a girl's parents are quick to notice if she shows any particularity, and anyway it's best to be above-board in all your dealings." Again, he felt a pang of guilt. "I'll tell you what," he added hurriedly. "My grandmother is, I believe, acquainted with this fellow Nash. I'll see if I can't get you an introduction to him, if you'd like."

There was little doubt that Elstow would like. His eyes positively goggling, he gasped, "J-John *Nash?* Oh, Leo! Could you? Would you? Oh, Gad! I do not know how to— What to—"

"For Lord's sake, stop babbling," exclaimed Savage, laughing. "Mrs. Hythe will say I've driven you into a delirium, and I shall be cast forth in disgrace! Now take my arm, and I'll help you downstairs. The ladies are likely waiting."

The ladies had not yet come down, however, and only Sir Everard was in evidence, hovering about Mrs. Netty in the kitchen, and begging samples from the various pans that bubbled and hissed and gave forth delicious fragrances.

"Welcome back to the land of the living, Elstow," he said in his amiable way. "We're to have a regular feast in your honour."

"Yes. At four o'clock," said Mrs. Netty, flapping a towel at them. "Now you must all go away, for no more samples will be forthcoming and I have work to do!"

They retreated to the withdrawing room where the afternoon sunbeams brightened a large Chinese urn filled with holly branches, and a fire crackled merrily on the hearth. A tray of decanters and glasses had been set on the credenza, and Savage carried a glass of Madeira to Elstow who had sunk gratefully onto the sofa.

"Jove, but this is jolly," said Paynton. "Be sorry to leave here, Leo. Be dashed if I won't. Though it's a pity the old abbey ain't—"

"Oh, Gad!" groaned Savage remorsefully. "I quite forgot to tell you, Pay. Mrs. Hythe has some truly splendid examples of armour and mail up at the abbey. I knew you'd be overjoyed to see them."

"What? Why, you villain! Fine armour and you didn't see fit to tell me? It don't say much for the state of your mind, or of your consideration for your oldest friend!"

Savage poured him a glass of brandy. "Here. Sluice this over your old ivories, ancient friend, and try to forgive my villainy. If you ask the Widow Hythe politely, she may allow you to view the antiquities tomorrow."

"I can scarce wait," exclaimed Paynton enthusiastically. "Might she let me buy some, do you suppose, Elstow? If they're fine, and mouldering away up among the ruins, I'd think—"

"No!" Elstow's response was sharp and vehement, and Paynton stared at him in surprise. "She—er, ain't allowed to," said the young man hurriedly, and in an obvious attempt to change the subject, asked, "In the meantime, when am I to see the famous henhouse?"

Much too well bred to press the issue, Paynton joined Savage who had crossed to stand by the fire. "It's in the barn until after you've viewed it," he said. "Then we plan to carry it outside and install the brutes. Might be rather a task, Leo. Lord knows, we made it solid enough to last a hundred years. Likely weighs a ton."

Savage said airily, "Oh, I've no doubt we'll manage, between . . ." His words trailed away.

The two ladies were coming down the stairs, side by side. Miss Underhill, all youthful innocence in a gown of pale green, drew an awed exclamation from Elstow, but Savage scarcely noticed her. If anyone had told him when first he saw Mrs. Hythe's spotted countenance, that she could look like this, he'd not have believed him. Her velvet gown was of soft blue, the low bodice trimmed with a band of beautifully worked embroidery that was repeated on the cuffs of the long sleeves. She wore pearl and sapphire earrings, and a matching pendant gleamed against the soft swell of her ample bosom. A blue ribbon was wound through her curls, and her bright eyes, meeting his incredulous stare, became even brighter, so that she blushed and lowered her lashes demurely.

Elstow had scrambled up and rushed to hand Miss Underhill down the remaining steps. Paynton, who had also moved very fast, bowed before the widow. "Ma'am," said he, offering his arm, "you put London's Toasts to shame, damme if you don't!"

Unutterably shocked, Savage thought, 'My God! She's a confounded beauty!' An imperative hand was tugging at his pantaloons. He blinked down numbly. A smaller beauty clad in pink and white, peered up at him. "Isn't him ever going to notice *her?*" she enquired with a plaintive sigh.

Savage took a steadying breath and swept her up.
"I was afraid," he said. "I didn't know if one was
permitted to talk to a princess."

She beamed on him. "We all getted dressed up,
'cause Brettoe's better an' we goin' to show him her
henhouse." She glanced at her mother who was apparently enthralled by something Paynton was saying. "Mama's prettiest of all," she observed.

He said slowly, "She most certainly is!" And it
occurred to him that Fate had dealt him a blow of
unparalleled vindictiveness.

Mrs. Netty carried in a teatray, and they enjoyed
a merry time together, during which it became obvious to Savage that he had erred in more ways than
one. If Paynton's very vulnerable heart had suc-
cumbed again, it was not the youthful loveliness of
the vicar's daughter that had conquered him, but the
sparkling beauty of an Unspotted Hythe. Listening
to that clear, laughing voice; watching the proud
carriage of her head, her grace as she poured the tea;
noting how intriguing was the generous shape of her,
how adorable the faint blush upon her (now) smooth
cheeks, and how revoltingly Paynton flattered and
flirted, Savage was alternately enchanted and infuriated. He betrayed neither emotion, however, nor
did anyone guess that by the time they all put on their
coats and went out to the barn, Leopold Byrne Savage had reached a somewhat ruthless decision on
how to deal with the vagaries of Fate.

THE BARN WAS CHILL on this winter afternoon, but it was still bright outside. When Savage swung the door open, both Elstow and Mrs. Netty stood rooted to the spot in astonishment.

"Good . . . God!" gasped Elstow, staring at the veiled bulk.

"Why, it is—enormous!" said Mrs. Netty. "I thought it was just for those two tiny little—"

"As well to prepare for the future, ma'am," explained Savage, one hand on the old sheets and blankets that shrouded their work of art. "Are we all ready?" Receiving assurances on this point, he and Paynton removed the covers.

Through a moment of stunned silence, Mrs. Hythe gazed at the most elaborately embellished and strangely contoured henhouse she had ever seen.

A band of intricate fretwork encircling the structure just under the eaves was painted bright yellow, while the rest of the house was a martial red. It appeared to stand about seven feet tall, but this was hard to determine since the rear wall, besides being narrower, was also some inches higher than the front, causing the peaked roof to tilt forward. The side walls of necessity sloped inward so as to connect with the back. The door in the front was panelled, and Mrs. Hythe was entranced to see that although it hung somewhat out of plumb, it boasted an obviously costly brass doorknob. Inside, a deep shelf was covered with straw, and two perches were polished to a gleaming finish. As a final touch, the roof boasted a gilded weather vane in the shape of a rooster.

Consuela broke the silence with a piercing squeal. Rushing to the henhouse, she hugged as much of it as she could reach, then began to dance round it, holding out her skirts and singing, "Her's got a henhouse! Her's got a henhouse!"

Mrs. Netty uttered a squawk and fled, covering her mouth with her apron.

His eyes filling with tears, Elstow declared heroically that he'd "Never seen one to equal it!"

Miss Underhill, less adept at concealing her feelings, whooped and giggled hilariously.

Very aware that a certain pair of blue eyes were fixed on her face, Mrs. Hythe battled a bubble of mirth, and said rather breathlessly that it was "a work of art," and, suspecting a dimple had escaped her, added, "The hens will be the proudest in all England when they are settled into their new home."

"And d'you like it, little miss?" asked Paynton, smiling at the ecstatic child.

"Oooh—yes!" she cried, interrupting her dance to hug his leg. "But whyzit smaller at the back?"

Paynton looked imploringly at his friend. Savage rose to the occasion, answering with bland sang-froid that it was designed to impress visitors with the fact that these hens were "exceptional."

Consuela jumped up and down several times and clapped her hands before remembering that Mr. Leo had not been given his hug. Having remedied this, she said sunnily, "Him put it outside now, so we put her chickys in."

Savage and Paynton exchanged a glance.

Mrs. Hythe said, "Oh, yes. Pray do. I have found just the right spot, where it will be shaded in summer and receive full light in wintertime. Unless," she added, arching her brows enquiringly, "you think we should get some strong labourers to carry it?"

Since neither Savage nor Sir Everard was prepared to admit the task beyond them, the ladies retired to the house while the gentlemen strove. They rested briefly when Savage split the back of his coat, and were obliged to rest again when Sir Everard's hand was caught and Savage momentarily lacked the strength to lift the henhouse sufficiently to free him. The air rang with their anguished profanity, which was as well, for it helped drown the faint sounds from the interior of the house where Mrs. Primrose, Miss Faith, and Mrs. Netty clung to each other and laughed until they wept.

At length, having dried her tears, Mrs. Primrose took pity on the builders and, going out to them again, ventured to suggest that if they could lift their masterpiece onto some of the discarded pieces of lumber (of which there were a great deal), they might gradually raise it until they could get the old barrow underneath and then wheel the house to its permanent location.

This was adjudged a capital notion and in no time the henhouse was lifted, rolled away, and settled.

Or approximately settled.

"Oh—er, dear," said Mrs. Primrose, blinking rather rapidly at the leaning work of art.

"Ground must be bent," gasped Sir Everard, faint and perspiring.

"Well, that's it, of course," agreed the widow, biting her lip to preserve her countenance.

"Ground straight," offered Consuela. "House bent."

Mrs. Netty, who had joined the small crowd to watch the final steps, went rushing off again, closely followed by Miss Faith.

Savage looked after them grimly.

"It's—ah, only that they are worried for—er, the joint," said Mrs. Primrose, apologetically.

"Are they." Savage gazed on the henhouse, covered his eyes and gave up. His laughter resounded through the gardens, and was at once joined by everyone else's until they all were weak and spent.

"Oh, Egad, Pay," Savage moaned, dabbing his cuff at his streaming eyes. "If there truly is 'talent in every branch of achievement' how can we have failed so lamentably?"

"No, no," said the widow comfortingly. "You both worked so very hard and—and did splendidly. But I fear the floor in that wretched barn is extreme uneven."

They were off again, and Elstow was obliged to sit down, exhausted.

Mrs. Netty and Miss Faith, who had come out to share the merriment, went away again, and returned escorted by an anxious Consuela, and carrying the box in which were the two exotic birds.

"Pop 'em in, poor brutes," sighed Sir Everard.

"Go home, Fred'rick," cooed Consuela as Mrs. Netty lifted a small and protesting chicken from the box. "Go home, Freda."

The adults eyed one another gravely, but no one smiled at the choice of names.

Everyone watched as corn was scattered inside, and the two small creatures squawked and scratched and pecked about.

"Why them not go on a' perch?" asked Consuela anxiously.

"Too busy stuffing 'emselves," answered Sir Everard.

A fluttering of wings, and Mrs. Primrose said, "There goes Frederick, darling."

"Freda," corrected her daughter. "Oh, there go Fred'rick." She clasped her hands her eyes radiant. "How lucky them are... to..."

While everyone gazed, fascinated, the two "lucky" birds slid slowly but inexorably down the slanting perch until they collided with the wall. With much squawking and flapping, they descended to the ground and rushed madly about.

Elstow pointed out weakly that perhaps if some boards were thrust under the right side, the house might be jacked up to the point that the perches were straight. This was accomplished. It was a faulted solution however, for no sooner was the desired result achieved than Frederick and Freda discovered there was now a suitable gap between the ground and the bottom of the right wall of their new home. Without a thought for the feelings of the men who had laboured so hard to provide them with private and luxurious accommodations, they shot under the wall and raced, squawking, back into the barn.

"Ungrateful brutes," grumbled Savage, and offered Mrs. Primrose his support as the again hilarious group adjourned to the house.

The celebration dinner was a great success, and afterwards the widow performed creditably upon her "pinafore." Paynton stood beside the spinet and turned the pages of her music, and when she played the beloved old folk songs everyone sang. Savage joined in heartily, but it seemed to Primrose that he avoided her eyes, and despite the warmth and fragrance of the room and the spirit of love that pervaded it, unease laid a shadow over her happiness.

CHAPTER SEVEN

PERHAPS BECAUSE his battered thumb was unexpectedly stiff and painful, Savage dropped the valise halfway down the stairs and cursed soft but fluently as it burst open and scattered his belongings about the hall. There came the shushing of feminine draperies and two slender hands flew to help him gather the tumbled articles.

"You are up early, ma'am," he said, thrusting undergarments hurriedly into the valise.

Keeping her eyes lowered, Mrs. Hythe restored a pigeon's feather to the handkerchief in which it had been carefully wrapped, and murmured, "Had you intended to slip away without saying goodbye, Mr. Savage?"

His lips tightened. He said in a rather gruff manner that he did not care for goodbyes.

The widow leaned back on her heels and met his eyes smilingly. "I should think you would be very glad for this one. What with being clawed, and worked to a shade, to say nothing of your poor hand—"

She paused as the "poor hand" closed over her own.

"You do not pull away," observed Savage, his voice very soft. "Is it possible that you are less afraid of me now?"

Lowering her eyes again, she said shyly, "You have given me no cause to be afraid, sir."

"Do you imply that someone has? If so, I would like to know who—and how."

"And why, and when?" In a swift graceful movement, she stood. She had paled, but her little chuckle rippled out and she said lightly, "La, sir, here is another melodrama. But if there *was* any fact to your fiction, and you possessed the answers to all those things, what would you do, I wonder? Call the evil wretch out and summarily despatch him? Does it not occur to you that the gentlemen of my family would have done so, had that been the case?"

"One would think they might have, certainly," he said, not noticing how nervously her hands had clenched, and frowning because he had spoken in earnest, and she seemed all coquettish mockery.

"Which should prove to you, Mr. Savage that the need did not arise. But indeed," she sank into a curtsey, "I thank your honour for the concern."

Irritated, he demanded baldly, "How long have you known Sir Conrad Furness?"

The widow was suddenly very still and very white. "Ah," she said in a breathless fashion. "Is...is *that* why you came here?"

"*What?* If you dare to imply that I came at his behest, my Gad, madam, I spy for no man!"

"Yet, you are his friend." Her chin tilted upward, and her mouth drooped scornfully. "And so *very* full of questions!"

"Which you are *so* reluctant to answer."

"You have no right to question me, Mr. Savage!"

His temper was up now, and refusing to acknowledge the truth of her statement, he said with freezing hauteur, "If I had questions, Mrs. Primrose, they were born of nothing more than a concern for the welfare of a lone woman."

"But how charming. And on such short acquaintance, too!"

His hand flashed out and caught her wrist. "Don't bandy words with me, my girl. Our acquaintanceship may be brief, but you and I have seen more of each other this past week than do many couples before they stand side by side at the altar."

She felt close to tears suddenly, but said, "Much good has it done you, for I think you have little gossip to relay to your bosom bow."

"Dammitall," said Savage grittily. "I was not aware you knew Furness 'til I met him on Tuesday! And—"

"Tuesday..." She wrenched free and turned her back on him. "I fancy he had plenty to say of the scandalous widow. And you believed whatever he told you."

"Of course I didn't believe him, but—"

"So he *did* talk about me! And you listened." She whirled to face him. "For shame, Mr. Savage! No, never deny it, for I noticed when you came back how strangely you looked at me. Now I know why!"

"Devil take it, I—"

"Oh, have done, sir! What is it to you if I was his mistress, or—"

"Mistress! Furness never said—"

"I care not what lies he told! Go, sir! Go and—and stop wasting your t-time here with—with Spotted Hythes, and—and chickens and ch-chicken-pox—"

"And crooked henhouses." His eyes twinkling, he reached out to her.

Blinded with tears, she did not see that gesture, and raged on, "I wish you might take the stupid thing with you! Perchance the lady your grandmama has...chosen for you, would be impressed by your carpentry, if by nothing—"

"No—Primrose, wait! I did not—"

"If by nothing else," she finished. And with a muffled sob and a flutter of skirts, she ran up the stairs and was gone.

Savage stared after her until Sir Everard came in from the kitchen, taking off his gauntlets and saying brightly, "Deuce take it, what a gruesome hour to be up and about, but I simply had to see the armour before we left. What a splendid collection! D'you think Mrs. Hythe could be persuaded to—" Here, catching sight of Savage's expression, he recoiled. "Oh, Egad! We've lost the war! Bonaparte is gobbling up frogs' legs in White's! Tell me what disaster has struck."

Savage took a deep breath and smiled. "Not struck, Pay. A disaster averted, more likely. Come, I'm famished. We'll take breakfast at The Merry Monk. Lord, but I'll be glad to leave this dashed desolation and get back to Town!"

Despite this declaration, Sir Everard noticed that his friend scarcely touched the large meal he ordered at the famous posting house, and that each time their conversation turned towards Erskine Abbey, Savage deftly turned it elsewhere.

"IT WILL BE THE TRIUMPH of the Season," said Lady Carlotta Hamildown, her crochet hook flying as she sat beside the fire in the morning room, with Tar snoring at her feet.

Leopold, who had overnighted at the family home on Grosvenor Place, rather than returning to his rooms on Sackville Street, pointed out that the ball would be ahead of the start of the Season, and might therefore be poorly attended.

"Flapdragon!" snorted her ladyship, fixing him with a smouldering eye. "Here—" she thrust her tangled skein at him. "Unravel this! Make yourself use— Why is your thumb bandaged?"

Nudging tentatively at the tortuous convolutions of the thread, he murmured, "It was struck with a hammer."

"The deuce! Who dared to attack you? And why so horrid a weapon?"

He grinned at her. "The hammer was in my own right hand, ma'am. And nowadays it is bad ton for a lady to swear."

Mr. Boswell Savage, who had been engrossed in the pages of *The London Gazette,* jerked his head up, and exclaimed in a tone of stark incredulity, "*You* held a hammer, Leo?"

"Quite apart from the fact that *anything* I do or say is good ton, impudent boy," declared her ladyship, "why in heaven's name were you holding such an object?"

"I found it difficult to construct a henhouse without one, ma'am."

Her ladyship dropped lace and crochet hook, and for once genuinely astonished, gawked at him.

Mr. Savage, who had risen and wandered over to stare at his son, laughed suddenly. "It is a hum, ma'am," he said. "He's hoaxing us."

"Not at all, sir." Restoring lace and crochet hook to his grandmother's lap, Leopold said, "I think you would be proud of my efforts, ma'am. It is a—er, splendid edifice."

"Good God," gasped Lady Carlotta. "He has gone demented! We had best cancel the ball, Savage. Your son's nursery would be inhabited by booberkins!"

"Why," enquired Mr. Savage, taking a cautious step closer to his amused offspring, "would you attempt such a vulgar task?"

"I did not merely attempt it, sir. It is *fait accompli* and awaiting only the singularly reluctant occupants."

"Foul!" cried her ladyship.

"If you spell that with a *w,* right you are, ma'am. And I undertook the task, sir, in an effort to repay my...landlady. Speaking of whom, Grandmama, do you know aught of the Hythe family?"

Lady Carlotta said fiercely, "I spell it with a *u,* rogue, because I do not care to be flimflammed! Building a henhouse, indeed! The day any Savage is obliged to construct shelters for livestock, will be the day that the British Empire collapses!"

"With all due respect, ma'am, there were savages building shelters for livestock, long before the British Empire came into being, so—" Laughing, he ducked the swipe of her fan, seized the shrunken old hand, and kissed it fondly. "My apologies for teasing the dearest of grandmamas. Now answer my question, I beg, for you know all there is to know about our noble families.''

Her fingers turned to caress his cheek, and, smiling, she said, ''You are up to mischief, Leopold Byrne Savage. I feel it in my poor old bones. But very well—Hythe, you say? Hmm... There are the Cardiff Hythes—very full of juice, but half of 'em are mad, and the other half went out to the Americas, Lord help 'em! The Americas, I mean, not the Hythes.''

''We are at war with America, ma'am,'' Mr. Savage pointed out gently.

''Well, it ain't to be wondered at, with the Hythes over there setting everything at sixes and sevens. Any self-respecting nation has a right to defend herself 'gainst such lummoxes!'' My lady waited until her convulsed grandson was quieter, then went on. ''There are the Leicestershire Hythes, of course. Far more respectable. A very ancient branch, and once well to do, but lost the fortune. A lot of it went with the South Sea Bubble, I believe. So many of our finest families were pauperized by that wicked fraud.''

Leopold said, ''But that was nigh a hundred years since, Grandmama.''

''Yes, and was the beginning of the end for the Hythes. After that, the estates were gradually sold or taken for debt 'til very little remained. It was sad, for the sons were the nicest creatures. I heard the younger—what on earth was his name? Oh, yes, Cyril—bought a farm somewhere and scratched out a living." She shuddered. "That aristocrats should come to such a pass! Dreadful! *His* only son was a great disappointment. Had a flair for art, and instead of going into the military as Cyril desired, went off and frippered about, and died in some godforsaken Italian hole, poor boy."

Sober now, Leopold asked intently, "Whereabouts is the farm? Do you know, ma'am?"

"In East Anglia, as I recall. Was it Norwich? No...Ipswich! That's it! Ipswich! Rascal? Where are you going?"

Leopold, who had come to his feet, bowed. "Thank you for your help, dear ma'am. Now, if you will forgive, I've an appointment. Sir," he turned to his father. "By your leave..."

"Do you dine here, scoundrel that you are?" enquired Lady Carlotta.

"My regrets, ma'am. When I return however, I will give myself the pleasure of calling on you."

"Will you! Well, it had best be *before* the ball! Mark me now, for I'll not forgive you if you fail to attend!"

THE MARCH SUNLIGHT added brightness if not warmth to the afternoon air. It was very clear and brisk, and from the hilltop on which Primrose had halted the cob she could see the glitter of the sea in

the southern distance, and closer at hand the hill
from which Erskine Abbey dominated the village.

If she looked very closely she could even discern
the gleam of the weather vane atop an ungainly little
structure purporting to be a henhouse. She gazed at
it sadly. How hard he had worked...and smashed his
poor thumb... And how they had laughed at the
unveiling; laughter in which he had joined like the
well-bred sportsman he was. To recollect the way the
darkly lashed blue eyes glinted when he was amused
caused her to turn her thoughts hurriedly in another
direction. It was useless, because a moment later she
was smiling wistfully as she saw again the stairs lit-
tered with his belongings; felt his warm hand closing over hers, heard his voice saying with such
gentleness, "Is it possible that you are less afraid of
me...?" She pulled herself together. She dared not
be less afraid of him! She must not remember his
many kindnesses, the occasional incredible tenderness in his eyes. It was better to dwell upon the proud
hauteur he could don like a mantle when it so pleased
him; the way he had ridden out of her life, tall and
straight, with not so much as a backward glance.

But the voices of memory would not be si-
lenced...

"When is Mr. Leo coming back, Mama...?"

"I find you very lovely indeed..."

"He's been gone two weeks, Prim. You'd think he
would at least have said goodbye..."

Goodbye...

"Cats are very fastidious, you know...I'll give him a bath tomorrow morning..."

A stifled sound somewhere between a sob and a laugh escaped her.

"Good day to you, Spotted Hythe."

"Spotted Hythe!" she muttered, wiping an impatient hand across her eyes. "Wretched man!"

"I might have guessed I'd not be welcomed in a friendly spirit!"

She jerked her head around. Leopold Savage, mounted on a beautiful black mare, was scant paces away, as elegantly at ease in the saddle as he was in the withdrawing room. She was vaguely aware of a superbly tailored frieze coat, the hat that was set at a jaunty angle on his dark curls, the corduroy breeches that hugged his shapely legs, and the mirror-like sheen of the grey-cuffed jockey boots. All this she glimpsed in a fleeting second, while most of her attention was on his rather grim smile, and the disturbing glitter in his eyes.

Instinctively, she gasped, "Mr. Savage! It *is* you!"

He took off his hat and bowed. "Are there others you designate as wretched men?"

"No! Yes! I mean— I thought— Oh, I did not hear you come."

"Not surprisingly, when you were so lost in thought." He glanced at the emerald sweep of meadows and woodland. "I see nothing to cause you to be melancholy. Unless— Ah, my unique venture into the building trade still stands, I see. But that should inspire admiration, not so sad a—"

"I was not melancholy," she lied, and indeed she felt far from melancholy at this particular moment. "How did you find me?"

He said with a grave smile, "It is just possible you know, ma'am, that I was simply out riding, and not seeking you."

"Oh," said Primrose, feeling her cheeks grow hot. "Well, of course, I—"

"On the other hand," he said, dismounting, "I might have seen you ride out as I approached the abbey. Allow me to help you down."

"Why? I must get back."

"Don't be petulant. Come. I wish to talk to you."

"I am not being petulant!" Her head tossed petulantly. "And we can talk on the way to the abbey."

"What makes you think I am going that way?" Her eyes flashed to him, bright with annoyance, and he chuckled and added disarmingly, "No, I must not tease you. Loveliest of unspotted widows, dismount I beg of you, for I've things to say that were best not said in front of others."

Her heartbeat becoming rather agitated, she relented and leaned to him, and he lifted her, his lips brushing her forehead as he set her down.

"Oh!" she exclaimed indignantly.

"What is it? Did you step on a stone?"

"You know perfectly well! You kissed me!"

"I did nothing of the kind! If my lips chanced to touch your brow, it was purely accidental. Furthermore, you have been sadly deprived if you fancy that to have been a fully accredited kiss. Such a caress should never be carelessly undertaken, but should proceed more like—"

She was jerked into his arms, and the wits she strove to gather were scattered because his lips found hers with bruising, terrible, intoxicating force. After an indefinite interval, "Like—that," he said somewhat breathlessly. "And you need not reproach yourself, for I don't begrudge time spent in enlightening you as to—"

Interrupting this wanton provocation, she tried to appear outraged. "I would ask how you dare so treat me, save that I know your bosom bow, and I can guess what he has said to destroy any respect you might otherwise hold for me."

"Your feather is crooked," said Savage maddeningly. "And your sentence, like most long periods, is muddled and lacks force. Aside from those regrettable lapses however, there is something you *cannot* guess, ma'am. To wit: I have been on a journey."

"Indeed?" Gritting her teeth, she straightened the feather in her small hat, and walked along beside him while remarking in a bored fashion that she really had very little time to spare.

"To East Anglia," he murmured.

The widow's pace faltered. "How...nice," she managed.

"Informative, at all events. And do you know, Mrs. Hythe, I met some of your relations there."

She gave a gasp and turned to face him, her face white and strained. "You are mistaken, s-sir."

"Evidently, I am. There can be no doubt but that the lady's deceased brother—one Ambrose Hythe— was your husband. But yet—for some strange reason she insists the gentleman never married."

Searching his face she found his eyes cold and hard now, his mouth set in an inflexible line. The reins fell from her hand. Clutching at his arm, she cried pleadingly, "Don't tell him! For the love of God! I *beg* you—don't tell him."

His lip curled. "But you yourself said that was why I came here, madam. Why should I not complete my, er...mission?" He sprang suddenly to throw an arm about her. "If you mean to faint...!"

She put a hand dazedly to her brow, and whispered, "No...I must not... Sir, is it asking too much to implore that you, a chivalrous gentleman, do not betray my secret?"

"Yes." He let her go abruptly. "Though I'll admit you did it very well. Try for the truth instead of your playacting, Unspotted Hythe."

She crouched, glaring at him. "Oh, but you are horrid," she advised through white clenched teeth. "Savage by name, and Savage by nature!"

He bowed. "You are not the first female to re-mark it. When you feel inclined I expect you will say something sensible."

"By what—right?" she demanded, fairly snort-ing at him. "By what *right* do you come here—spy-ing for your loathsome crony? By what *right* dared you go snooping and prying all over East Anglia to discover something that is—that cannot possibly be of concern to you? By what *right* do you demand that I tell you of—of personal matters involving only my family?"

He looked at her impassioned face and drawled coolly, "Do you want me to convey to my—er, loathsome crony that you never married Ambrose Hythe?"

The widow wilted. Her proud head bowed, and her hands went up to cover her face. She said in muffled despair, "No."

"Then I shall require convincing, Mrs.—er, *Miss* Primrose."

"To think," she whispered, "that I ever fancied you to be...a gentleman...."

He grasped one small hand and slapped her reins into it. "Good day, madam," he said, turning away. "I gave you a chance."

"No! No—wait!" She lifted a tear-streaked face. "If I tell you what you want to know, will you at least grant me a little time to get Consuela away be-fore you—tell him?"

For a moment Savage stared at her, his face enig-
matic. Then he said, "I shall promise nothing until
I know the full details." He led the way to a sunny
spot out of the wind, where he tied the reins to some
bushes so that the horses could graze, then spread his
frieze coat for Mrs. Hythe to sit on. "Now," he said,
taking his place beside her. "Let us have it from the
beginning, if you please. When did you meet Furness?"

The widow moistened pale lips, and stared blindly
at the horses. "Seven years ago," she commenced
with low-voiced reluctance. "I was seventeen. Papa
was alive then, and had taken my sister Katherine
and me to a party in Brighton. Furness was there,
quite the dashing man about Town, and much pet-
ted, yet he paid me a flattering degree of attention."

"And you fell in love? He's a handsome fellow, I
own, but surely, he is a good deal older than you?"

"He is, but that is not why—far from falling in
love—I took him in strong dislike. Katherine was the
beauty of the family, and I was sure he was only cul-
tivating my acquaintance so as to tease her."

"Knowing Furness," said Savage, "I'd fancy he
would pursue the lady he wanted and not waste his
time with devious games."

"He wasted his time insofar as I was concerned,
certainly, but I was quite unable to discourage him.
When he became offensive, I had to appeal to my
father. Papa was incensed, for Sir Conrad should

have approached him, of course, before ever trying
to fix his interest with me. It was no use, however.
The man is so puffed up with his own consequence
that he refused to believe I did not find him the most
handsome and desirable gentleman in London Town.
I cannot express to you how deep was my astonishment when he formally offered for my hand, nor
how intense was his rage when his offer was refused.
I think he had never before been denied what he
wanted.''

Savage said with obvious scepticism, ''Even so,
Conrad Furness is a gentleman. I find it difficult to
believe that he continued to court you, over your
father's objections.''

''Then by all means do not strain your credulous-
ness, sir,'' she said bitterly, ''for he ceased his per-
secution. For a long while, I imagined myself safe. I
did not go about much, for Papa had suffered a
small stroke and liked to have me by him.'' She bit
her lip, then said slowly, ''But Kate was— Well, she
was very lovely, and always some gentleman or other
was escorting her. Mama indulged her, and neither
of us dreamed...'' She shrugged. ''Your gentle-
manly bosom bow, Mr. Savage, is a vindictive man.
He persuaded Kate to... to elope with him.''

''The devil he did! Furness has never married.''

''They were married by a travelling divine in Italy.
You may believe it was never published in England.
We did not hear from Kate for over a year. Then

Mama received a letter—a most pitiful thing. Kate had very soon discovered that the marriage was a farce, staged to avenge the 'insult' her family had dealt him. He had hired an actor to perform the 'ceremony.' Kate was expecting a child, and when she became what he termed 'unsightly,' he abandoned her.''

For a moment Savage was silent. Then he asked, ''Who fought him?''

She looked at him steadily. ''Who would you suppose? My father had suffered a second stroke when Kate eloped. He was bedridden. My brother fell with Lord Nelson at Trafalgar. Cousin Barrett was only a boy, but had he known, he would have at once rushed to Italy and challenged Furness.''

''And have been shot out of hand. Yes. Conrad is a skilled duellist. But do you tell me, madam, that you are not acquainted with any gentlemen who would have called Furness to account were these alleged and appalling—er, facts made known?''

''We could not make the facts known.'' She saw his right eyebrow arch upward and a cynical smile curve his mouth, and suddenly it was vital that he not believe ill of her. ''Katherine was terrified lest Furness find out about the entail. She begged that Mama go to her, but my father was failing rapidly. Mama dared not leave him, or let him know the truth, so we told him I had been invited to visit Kate, and I went to Madrid.''

He stared at her. "Alone? Egad, you are a resourceful woman, ma'am."

"Of course not alone! Mrs. Netty was my chaperon."

"I see. What was there about the entail that your sister wished to keep from Furness?"

"It is an unusual one. The property is left to the eldest living male heir. If there be no male heir, however, it reverts upon the eldest living—heir of the body, and only if there is no such person does it go to the nearest male relative."

"Unusual, indeed! So at your father's death, your sister would inherit?"

"Yes. The abbey, as you have seen, is sadly dilapidated. But some of the works of art are extreme valuable, and can be sold only at the discretion of the holder of the entail. None of my ancestors was willing to part with our belongings. Papa, out of desperation, did sell two paintings but only so as to enable Katherine and me to have proper come-outs."

"And your sister was afraid that if Furness discovered she was an heiress... But, surely, he would then have returned to her."

"He did exactly that," she said dryly. "He must have been on his way back to her when she posted her letter to Mama. Kate lived in terror of him, for he had treated her vilely. She was all alone when he arrived, and it was easy for him to force her into solemnizing their marriage vows. Then he rushed back

to England again to see Papa. By the time I reached
Kate she was half out of her mind for fear that her
child would suffer the kind of misery she had endured. Two weeks later we had word from Mama
that my dear father had died, and that the solicitors
had notified Sir Conrad of the terms of the entail. By
the very next post Kate received a letter from him—
full of sympathy and affection. He was flying to her
side, he said, to be with her at the birth of their
child.''

He frowned. ''So you married Hythe to provide
yourself and your sister with a protector.''

''Quite wrong, sir. No one could protect Katherine or her child against the villain who was now her
legal husband. Netty and I bore my poor Kate off to
Milan, where I had friends. The journey was hard,
and each time another coach appeared Kate was terrified that Sir Conrad had caught us. The doctor in
Milan told me that—that he feared for her mind.
And that he very much doubted she would survive
the birth.'' She shook her head sadly. ''My poor sister. So lovely, and so wilful... She knew that she was
dying. She used to lie in my arms, weeping, begging
me to hide her helpless little baby, not to let Furness
take it. I swore on my father's memory that I would
never let such a thing happen, and I wracked my
brains trying to find an answer. At last, as if it were
a gift from heaven, it came to me.''

''In the form of Ambrose Hythe?''

She nodded. "My friends were acquainted with him, and he dined often at the house. He was a fine artist, but he had alienated his father by coming to Italy to study. He was almost out of funds, and he was of a consumptive habit. I laid my problem before him, and he agreed at once to help us. We used my jewellery to pay his bills. He was a kind young man, and meant to keep his word, but—alas, we could not find a Protestant divine in Milan to marry us. Ambrose announced to everyone that we had been secretly married some months earlier, and I wrote to Mama with the same tale. Soon afterwards, Kate gave birth prematurely. By morning, she was . . . dead."

"You never— By God, you did! You took her child! How the deuce did you get away with it?"

"I still had one piece of jewellery left. Ambrose used it to bribe the physician to issue a certificate that Kate's child was stillborn. We took the baby and moved to Rome, telling everyone Consuela was our own child. We hoped to be married there, but the one divine we found refused to marry us because he said we were living in sin." She smiled wryly. "Poor Ambrose was much too ill to justify such an accusation, besides which he was a true gentleman and had never once taken advantage of our situation. Netty and I looked after him. I found a position in the salon of a famous modiste where my knowledge of English was useful, and Mama sent us what funds she could manage. Ambrose went to his reward when Consuela was eighteen months old, and we came home."

Savage, looking very grim, said, "Then Furness still doesn't know the little girl is his own."

"He believes she was born to Ambrose and me. Out of wedlock. But he has never forgiven me. Whenever any gentleman has shown the least interest, your friend has lost no time in blackening my reputation."

"Which you fully deserve, Miss Primrose," said Savage harshly.

Her eyes flew to him. She had hoped against hope that her sad tale would move him to compassion. To see his eyes ablaze and his mouth harsh with anger wrought havoc with her heart, and although she strove for the strength to quarrel with him, she found that all she could do was fight back a flood of tears.

"If there was a particle of truth in the tragedy you have related, you need not have concealed a word of it," Savage went on. "You could have denounced such a blackguard without danger to yourself, or to your niece."

"What...stuff!" Furious, she dashed away the tears that beaded on her lashes. "He knew I took Kate to Milan. He could have claimed that I influenced her to run away from him, whereof she died! Besides, who would listen to a disgraced woman who lived in Europe for two years with a gentleman to whom she was not wed? Furness could claim Con-

suela and take her away, and God help the poor mite
if he did so! He is her legal father and is in desperate
financial straits. He would do anything to claim the
inheritance. No, and no! I had sooner spend the rest
of my life running away than let her fall into his
clutches!''

He sat there glowering at her, and after a minute
she asked cautiously, ''Dare I hope that you will not
betray my confidence, Mr. Savage?''

A long pause, and then he growled, ''On one condition, ma'am.''

''Wh-which is . . . ?

He stood and pulled her to her feet, and then went
over to untie the reins. ''I am obliged to attend that
wretched ball my sire and my conniving grandmama
have arranged. I want you to come with me.''

Beginning to tremble, she said, ''For—for what
purpose, sir?''

''Give me your foot.'' He threw her up into the
saddle. ''To be my partner, of course.''

''You must be mad!'' she gasped, astounded.
''Have you understood nothing I said? I am notorious! Your father and your grandmama would be enraged!''

''Quite so.'' He swung gracefully into the saddle
and reined the mare around as she pranced play-
fully. ''It might serve to teach them never to try to
force my hand again.''

Primrose stared at him. "Would you subject me to such humiliation only to best your family?"

"You are unfair, ma'am. I merely propose a trade. My silence in exchange for your cooperation in a small prank. The choice, of course, is yours."

The Widow Hythe took a deep breath. "You use the wrong word, Mr. Savage," she said bitterly. "It is not a choice. It is blackmail."

"The trouble with you," said Leopold Savage, "as I have remarked before, is that you want for a proper sense of gratitude."

CHAPTER EIGHT

"LEO, YOU RASCAL!" Peter Cliveden came into the library of Cliveden House, shooting his cuffs and hurrying to greet his friend. "What devilry are you about now?" Despite this unamiable greeting, affection shone in his grey eyes, and following their strong handshake he gave Savage a hearty clap on the back.

A parlourmaid passing the door glanced in and sighed dreamily, and indeed they presented an impressive picture of young manhood, Cliveden being clad in regimental evening dress, and Savage's long-tailed coat and knee breeches as if molded to him.

A tall young man with light brown hair, a humorous mouth and a strong chin that belied his slight build and quiet manner, Cliveden was related to Savage through the marriage of his wife's brother to Geraldine, Leopold's only sister. Once rivals in love, they had formed a friendship which had survived some severe trials and deepened to the point that it was no longer necessary that they be polite to each other. Demonstrating this, Savage raised a jewelled quizzing glass and scanned Cliveden critically.

"Well, aren't we as fine as fivepence," he drawled, sitting down again. "I don't wonder that you haul your regimentals out of mothballs for these grand occasions, Peter. There's nothing will draw the ladies' eyes faster. Dare I trust that, although your lovely wife is in the country, you have kept the line with my widow?"

Cliveden, who had left the army after having been badly wounded at Badajoz the previous year, grinned and said, "If I was tempted to overstep it, you can scarce blame me. Mrs. Hythe is a beautiful creature. Why in the deuce she does not stay with your grandmama, I cannot fathom."

"Because Lady Carlotta would not have her in the house. Frightfully bad ton, you know. Quite notorious."

Cliveden's smile was replaced by a look of dismay and a gathering frown. "You didn't tell me that."

"I hope I am not such a fool. Your august sire would never have allowed her to come here, and I had to have a respectable house where she could stay."

"There are such things as hotels, you know."

"Wouldn't serve, dear boy. Under the circumstances." Cliveden's lips tightened, noting which Savage murmured with a faint smile, "Don't get frosty. I did take Lady Ian into my confidence."

"My mother knows? She said nothing of it to me."

"Of course. Her ladyship does not break her given word."

Cliveden stared at him, then gave a reluctant laugh. "Damn you, Leo! Why must you always go from Brighton to Bristol to get to Whitehall?"

Savage chuckled. "Because it amuses me to see you don your austere look. Now, tell me what you really think of the widow."

"She is delightful, and very pretty mannered. The General is most taken with her, and I know mama has enjoyed having her here. Indeed, I'd fancy you were hoaxing me with this bad ton business, save that . . ." He hesitated.

His blue eyes very keen under their drooping lashes, Savage prompted, "Don't hesitate to plant me a facer."

Cliveden said, "No—nothing of a derogatory nature. Only that I sometimes think she is very unhappy."

"Lord! Has she been a watering pot? I'd not have thought it of—"

"I hope I have not been so," said a clear voice from the doorway. "Have I, Mr. Cliveden?"

The gentlemen sprang to their feet. Cliveden was scarlet with embarrassment, but Savage merely stared, putting up his quizzing glass again.

The Widow Hythe wore a ball gown of rose satin overlaid with white lace. The very décolleté neckline was heart-shaped; a single strand of pearls shone against the snowy swell of her bosom, and was complemented by ruby and pearl earrings. Her hair was swept into a cluster of curls high on her head. A zephyr shawl trimmed with Brussels lace was draped about her shoulders, and the hand she extended as she came into the room was encased in a long white glove.

"No—indeed! N-never, ma'am," stammered Cliveden, bowing over her fingers.

"I am so glad." She smiled at him warmly. "It would be a poor return for your kindness." As she turned to Savage, the warmth of her smile vanished. "Well, sir? Lady Cliveden helped me select the gown. Does it suit? I warn you it was costly."

For a moment he continued to stare at her. Then he shrugged. "If it serves the purpose, the investment is well made. Come, we are sufficiently tardy. My grandmama will be eager to rend me when I arrive with a partner."

When they reached Lady Hamildown's great house on Curzon Street, however, beyond giving Savage a grim stare, bestowing a smile on Cliveden, and looking keenly at Mrs. Hythe, her ladyship did not seem unduly provoked. It was Mr. Savage who, having greeted the widow politely, murmured, "A word with you later, my boy," his eyes shooting anger.

They made their way through the crush around the reception area, Savage and Cliveden responding

merrily to the many friends who accosted them, and
the widow maintaining a calm demeanour in the face
of male admiration and feminine curiosity, resentment, or condescension.

Guiding her towards the ballroom, Savage murmured, "You have bowled everyone out, ma'am. All
eyes are on you."

She was uneasily aware of this. "Yes, I could see
that your father was overjoyed, and you may be sure
Lady Hamildown will be properly bowled out when
she discovers my reputation. What will you do if she
asks you to take me away?"

"Oblige her," he answered promptly. "It would
enable me to escape this wretched matrimonial mi-
asma! Oh, God! Here comes Mrs. Cutterleigh, prepared to offer up the last of her brood. She knows
the chit cannot abide me!"

He bowed to the ample dowager, and Miss Cutterleigh fluttered long eyelashes and looked demure,
betraying no sign of the aversion he had claimed.

Cliveden led the widow into the quadrille that was
forming up. "I must seize my chance now," he said
kindly, "for there'll be no room on your dance card
after this."

Primrose smiled, but she knew that she was here
for but one purpose, to punish Savage's grandmama
and his sire, and her heart failed her when she
thought of what the evening might bring.

Cliveden had told her apologetically that he was not an accomplished dancer, but he made such an obviously great effort to move correctly through the measures that she could not fail to be both touched and amused. When he escorted her from the floor, mopping his brow and groaning that he had likely disgraced her, she laughed and told him that he had done exceeding well.

"One thing," he said with a grin, "it's probably the last time you'll have to endure my clumsiness, ma'am. Only look."

The widow was astonished to find a regular bevy of gentlemen waiting to be introduced, and more astonished when her dance card was rapidly filled. Savage had already put his own name in the slot for a minuet and told her he meant to take her in to supper at its conclusion.

Long before the orchestra struck up for the minuet, however, Mrs. Hythe's nightmare had begun. She was dancing with Sir Everard Paynton, his obvious admiration having lulled her fears, when she glimpsed a scowl on his face. It vanished in an instant and his smile was as charming as ever, but glancing to the side she saw several ladies whispering behind their fans while they watched her. Her heart gave a sickening lurch. As the pair proceeded through the dance, the hand she extended in the various exchanges was often merely brushed, rather than clasped. The eyes of the ladies looked over or through her; the smiles of some gentleman acquired a fixed quality.

She was trembling when the music stopped. Leading her from the floor, his mouth unwontedly grim, Sir Everard changed direction and commandeered two glasses of champagne from the tray of a waiter. Confused, Primrose realized suddenly why they had turned aside. Savage was one of a small group gathered about Sir Conrad Furness. The handsome baronet was talking in a low voice, but a sudden flurry of shocked exclamations rang out, and all heads turned in the direction of the widow. Feeling the blood drain from her cheeks, she saw Savage's hand rest on Sir Conrad's shoulder as he murmured something. Sir Conrad gave a howl of mirth, then, obviously repeating the remark, reduced the other members of the group to sly giggles and subdued hilarity, while once again many eyes turned to her, some with curiosity, most with contempt.

Primrose looked down at the glass she held. It was shaking. She bit her lip hard, and fought for steadiness.

"So there you are." The deep voice sent a pang through her. She whirled to face Savage, prepared to demand that he take her home, but his eyes were on Paynton. "Been looking for you, dear boy," he said smilingly. "My revered grandmama requests your attention. You'll excuse us, ma'am, I feel sure."

The thought of being left alone in that room full of people who were gossiping about her, despising her, reduced the widow's knees to blancmange. "No!" she said sharply. "Mr. Savage, you must not—"

But they were already walking away, Savage's hand tight on his friend's elbow as he murmured something in an amused voice.

Primrose felt like a scullery maid abruptly transported to the middle of a coronation ceremony in Westminster Abbey. Wherever she looked now, were condemning glances, angry whisperings. Fans fluttered, gentlemen "Pshaw-ed" and looked affronted. She made her way slowly, and she hoped with dignity, towards some chairs. The ladies she passed turned their backs. The people sitting nearby arose at once and moved away. She had seldom been more relieved than when the music struck up for the minuet. He would come now. She would demand that he take her away so that she could escape this horrid trap he had put her in. Other ladies were being led to the floor; a burst of chatter and laughter mingled with the light melody. But Mr. Leopold Savage was talking with his grandmother and a giggling bevy of beauties, and neither looked in her direction or took one step towards her.

Two ladies paused nearby. "...would *I* do?" trilled one. "My dear, I hope you know I would never sink to such conduct. But if I had—I would slink out of this house, as fast as possible.''

''And return to the kennel whence you came, my love?''

''Just so, dearest. No, *really,* can you *credit* that such a trollop would dare...''

Primrose began to feel sick. 'Oh, Leo,' she thought, agonized. 'How *could* you? How *could* you?'

The entry hall seemed miles away, but at length she came to her feet, and wandered towards it. For every step there was a cruel giggle, a slurring remark, but she kept her head up somehow. And suddenly, a small elderly lady wearing a magnificent diamond tiara was before her. A shrill, autocratic voice was saying fiercely, ''...to bring that—that immoral *baggage* to the ball I planned for you! How *dare* you, sir?''

Savage's lazy voice contained a quiver of amusement. ''Now Grandmama, you said yourself she was a pretty creature, and with an air—''

''Aye! The air of the gutter!''

''I'll own that had I been fully aware of her—er, disgraceful repute—''

''You are aware now, sir! Remove her! And I shall not wish to see your face until—''

''Your pardon, madam.'' Sir Everard Paynton's voice sounded hardly his own, it was so clipped and angry. ''Mrs. Hythe. May I be of service?''

Lady Hamildown turned, her chin up, her eyes flashing wrath.

A sudden seething rage possessed the Widow Hythe. She said clearly, "I believe Mr. Savage must have forgotten that he signed for this dance."

Lady Hamildown gasped. "Of all the impertinence—"

Savage turned and put up his quizzing glass, surveying Primrose with a trace of condescension. "Dear lady, if that is so, I am assured you will find it to be a forgery. I signed for the Roger de Coverley, not the minuet."

Primrose jerked up her dance card. Her horrified eyes travelled down the list. It was truth. Sir Reginald Barrows had signed for the minuet and had evidently decided not to claim it. Beside the Roger de Coverley was Savage's familiar scrawl. Numbed, she thought, 'Oh no! Dear Lord—no!' She looked pleadingly into his bored smile. "Leo...you wouldn't! Please—take me home."

"As you wish, dear ma'am." He excused himself to the frigid statue that was his grandmother, and took Primrose's arm. Leading her towards the hall, he murmured, "But you will forfeit your bargain, you know."

She halted, looking up at his gentle smile. "You *promised!*"

"Quite true. Our bargain was that you attend this ball in exchange for my silence. And the ball is not over yet."

Fighting sobs, she said, "But—you have seen how they all despise me!"

"Indeed. I counted on it."

"Leo—for the love of God! I *cannot!*"

"But only think, dear lady. The beauty of the Roger de Coverley is that it includes *everyone.* In that way they will *all* see who I brought here tonight."

She had a sudden sickening picture of the long line of couples facing each other; of the changing of partners, each end pair dancing the cross-over through the centre from one end to the other, until all had completed; the parade through the arch. And she whispered despairingly, "Oh! How they would hate having to dance with me! I—cannot! Have mercy, I beg you. Your grandmama is sufficiently angry—can you not be content?"

He considered this. "It might serve. But—a bargain is a bargain, Widow Hythe. You must make your choice..."

Primrose closed her eyes briefly. Opening them, she looked at him with disgust. "Very well, Mr. Savage. I'll not break my word. But—I see that Sir Conrad Furness has chosen well in naming you friend!"

He bowed, and with an ironic smile took her back into the ballroom where he very soon left her again.

For the next hour, Primrose stood at the side in lonely state. The gentlemen who had signed her dance card had apparently quite forgotten having done so, and she watched stonily as the colourful dancers whirled and chattered while she might have been invisible. After a while, Peter Cliveden hurried to her side. From the corner of her eye she had seen Savage attempt to detain him. The young man was pale, his eyes sparking wrath, but he summoned a tight smile and asked if she would wish to join the dance.

Primrose could not know how deathly pale was her face or how touching her attempt at dignity. She looked up at him and said quietly, "You should not risk your reputation by speaking with me, Mr. Cliveden. Much less by dancing with me."

"They are—insufferable," he exclaimed. "And as for Leo Savage—! Madam, I believe we once were warned to be careful in casting 'the first stone.' I for one, could not dare do so. It will be my honour to lead you into the dance. Unless you wish to be escorted home-for which I'd not blame you. Be da— dashed if I'd not as soon leave m'self!"

Warmed by his kindness, she thanked him. "But, unhappily, sir, I have made a promise and cannot break it."

Seconds later, a footman brought him a message that General Sir Ian Cliveden desired his immediate presence in the library. Primrose had already dis-

covered that Peter idolized his distinguished father,
and although he apologized for the necessity of
leaving her, and vowed to return at once, she did not
see him again.

She felt drained of all emotion by the time the
Roger de Coverley was announced, but the worst was
yet to come. The whisperings, the shocked glances as
an unsmiling Leopold Savage led her onto the floor
were not hidden now. The music struck up. Primrose's knees were wobbling dangerously, but she
struggled through the initial measures. And suddenly, she stood opposite a most elegant young
dandy who sneezed violently and even as she reached
out to him, backed away, burying his face in a handkerchief. The lady beside him tossed up her head,
and left the dance with him. And on each side of
Primrose were empty spaces. The music faltered and
stopped. The scene blurred before Primrose's eyes,
and only a rageful determination not to allow Savage to claim she had not fulfilled the terms of the
bargain, kept her from picking up her skirts and
running away from this nightmare. Savage put up his
quizzing glass and looked about. Nobody seemed to
notice that anything was amiss, the ladies and gentlemen stood about conversing merrily, but the dance
had ended almost before it began.

"Dear me," said Savage, and extended his arm. "I
think we may call our bargain sealed, ma'am. Ah,

Cliveden, be so good, will you, old boy? I believe Mrs. Hythe is feeling indisposed.''

Before Cliveden could respond, Savage had wandered off in the direction of Sir Conrad Furness.

As a silent Peter Cliveden escorted the notorious widow from the ballroom, Primrose heard the outburst of sly giggles and a rising tide of malicious laughter.

She contained herself until they were safely in the carriage, but as it started to roll along the wide thoroughfare, her restraint broke. She bowed forward, and burst into a storm of weeping.

Horrified, but ever the gentleman, Cliveden gathered her into his arms and patted her shoulder, striving to comfort her. "There, there, dear ma'am. It is why I seldom venture into the ton, dashed if it isn't. They're a beastly cruel lot of—"

Her head jerked up. The light from the carriage lamps shone like silver ribbons on the tracks tears had left on her cheeks. "I care not for—for them," she sobbed. "It is *him!* The horrid, *horrid* brute!" Her little hands pounded against the blameless Cliveden's chest. "Oh! Oh! How I—*hate,* and *loathe,* and *despise* the wretched creature!

"Ow...!" whispered Peter Cliveden.

SIR EVERARD PAYNTON sauntered for the fourth time round the square, his anxious gaze flashing to the fine old mansion that had been the home of the

Furness family for the past hundred years. The marble steps were still unoccupied. He swung his cane over his shoulder and told the iron railings beside him some home truths about loyalty to one's friends. He stopped as the front door opened, then hurried his steps.

Leopold Savage sauntered down to join him.

"Well?" asked Paynton.

"Not so well," murmured Savage. "There's an execution in the house, Pay."

"Good God! Not a bailiff, surely?"

"Large as life, installed in the front hall. Poor old Conrad don't like it above half."

"So I should think. He'll be relying heavily on the match tomorrow. But—never mind that." Scanning his friend's face, he said, "You're sweating, dear boy."

"Do try not to be vulgar." Savage drew his handkerchief and dabbed at his lips. "Commoners sweat. A gentleman perspires. You know, Pay," he went on musingly, "I sometimes think it would be jolly good to be a commoner."

Paynton stared at him. "What did he say?"

"Commoners," said Savage, warming to his theme, "are much maligned, dear boy. Yet only look at the interesting life they lead. They are permitted to have a trade—to fill up their days *doing*, and achieving. You and I and our ilk are forbidden to do anything. I really may have to *do* something."

"Devil take it! What, for instance?"

"Well, since I have mastered the carpenter's art, I thought I might study. Snakes, perhaps. Did you know that there is a specimen in the Americas called a rattlesnake? It warns its prey before it strikes. Nobody likes the creature, because it's rather deadly. But, it seems to me that it plays fair." He met his friend's gaze levelly. "It would behoove a gentleman to emulate such an example, do you not think?"

Paynton blinked. "I fancy there must be a lot of dead rattlesnakes."

"So I was told."

Catching his arm, Paynton demanded in an unwontedly harsh tone, "What did he *say?*"

"Exactly what I had expected. Everything the widow said was untrue. A pack of lies, in fact. As if any man of breeding would sink so low. Poor old Conrad was—quite upset. One can scarce blame him." Savage smiled suddenly and clapped his friend on the back. "What a good fellow you are, Pay. And so acute. Would that I had listened to you."

"Very likely, but you won't listen to me now," grumbled Paynton. "You and your stupid damned rattlesnakes!"

"BUT THEN..." sandy-haired Lord Blainville paused dramatically and the large and crowded lounge of The Sportsman was hushed, the members of The Liars' Club waiting expectantly. "She turned up the

lamp," he went on, "and saw that—his hair was—
red!" A brief pause, then the room rang with
whoops and howls of laughter.

"His hair . . . was . . . *red,* begad!" wheezed Major
Tobbington of the Guards.

"Oh—rare!" chortled Mr. Redditch, coming near
to impaling his cheek on his shirt point. "You shall
have your work cut out to best that one, Savage—or
you either, Furness."

"Well, there's no time like the present," said Sir
Everard Paynton, his smile oddly strained as he
turned to Savage. "Shall you hold for the last position, Leo? Or do you yield that to Furness?"

Savage rose, yawned politely, and agreed to yield
the final position. Sauntering to the dais from which
they were all obliged to offer their tales, he scanned
the assembled gathering through his quizzing glass.
There were noticeably fewer smiles than usual, and
he knew that he was still in disgrace both for having
violated proper manners by escorting Mrs. Hythe to
his grandmother's ball, and for having declined to
honour his obligation by taking her home.

He also knew the value of suspense, and took his
time with the scrutiny.

An irked rear-admiral demanded, "Come along
do, Savage. We don't propose to wait all night! Let's
hear you try and throw dust in our eyes!"

With a faintly self-satisfied smile, Savage lowered
the glass. "No such thing, sir," he protested. "I

mean to be straight and above-board with you. No cozening from me this afternoon, I promise."

"If that's your lie," said Mr. Redditch, "it's a damned good one, Leo!"

There was much laughter, then Paynton, who was this year's Moderator, held up his hands and quiet was restored.

"My tale begins," said Savage in his lazy drawl, "as all good tales should, with a beautiful young damsel, who was as foolish as she was lovely, and therefore much desired." He waited out some hoots and applause, then went on: "She had, however, a younger sister. Not as beautiful, or very foolish, but—spirited, gentlemen. And therefore, just as desirable. Now this sister, whom I shall call Rose, fell under the eye of a gentleman about London Town. A dashing fellow, blessed with a fine old name, good looks, an insinuating address, a fine physique and a respectable fortune. He was older than Rose, and had acquired some reputation of being an—er, amateur libertine."

He was obliged to pause for more laughter and, smiling indulgently around his audience, saw from the corner of his eye that Sir Conrad Furness stood very still, watching him intently.

"Sir Libertine," he resumed when quiet was restored, "was so enamoured of the fair Rose that, although her dowry was small, he very generously offered her marriage. No one could have been more

surprised than he, when she refused. He was convinced, in fact, that she was playing the coquette, and
he continued to pursue her until her father was
obliged to request that he cease his unwelcome at-
tentions." He lifted his quizzing glass, turned to Sir
Conrad, who was now rather white about the mouth,
and winked. Furness started, and looked away, but
that conspiratorial wink had not gone unnoticed, and
several gentlemen nudged each other.

"You might think this ended the matter," drawled
Savage, "but Sir Libertine was of a vengeful nature.
His consequence had suffered a telling blow. He decided to punish the family, and he accomplished this
by persuading the beautiful elder daughter, whom I
shall call Kitty, to elope with him."

Some frowns appeared now, and Lord Blainville
said, "Don't think I much care for your Sir Libertine, Savage."

"Pshaw," snorted the admiral. "The fellow married the silly chit, certainly."

"Couldn't do anything else," agreed a stout middle-aged baronet. "She was a lady of Quality, after
all. Eh, Leopold?"

"She was, sir. And for all her silliness, a gentle
creature. He did wed her. And not until almost a year
later—by which time she was in a delicate condition—did he tell her that the priest who had performed the ceremony was in reality an unemployed
actor."

"The devil!" cried Paynton, as many shocked exclamations rang out. "And she a lady of Quality? You paint us a thorough blackguard!"

Again, Savage turned his quizzing glass to Sir Conrad Furness, where it remained as he said, "So I think. Do you all agree, gentlemen?"

Again, there was a ripple of speculation, and several low-voiced exchanges.

Furness shrugged with poised nonchalance, but his handsome features were flushed and his eyes gleamed dangerously. "A very unlikely tale, old boy. But it is, after all, make-believe."

"True enough," agreed Lord Swann, whose usually sleepy eyes were now bright and alert. "Pray go on, Savage. I find your tale—" he locked glances with Furness, whom he loathed, "—uncommon interesting."

So Savage went on, his calm unemotional voice adding weight to the tragedy which he related just as Primrose had told him. When he reached the point at which Primrose had taken Katherine's child whom the father believed to be stillborn, Furness gave an audible gasp. Savage turned to see his face contorted and almost purple, and for a moment thought he was about to be attacked, but again the baronet controlled himself. The small by-play had not gone unnoticed, however, and as Savage resumed his tale the eyes of many men were turned on Furness.

For a moment after Savage finished speaking, nobody moved, and the room was wrapped in a
breathless hush.

"Egad, sir," breathed Sir William Wansford.
"Your Sir Libertine is more like to a monster!"

"I'd like to get my hands on the dirty bastard—did
he exist," agreed Lord Swann, his grim stare fixed on
the livid Furness.

"And is that the end of your tale, Leopold?" enquired Mr. Boswell Savage, watching his son
shrewdly. "This brave lady brought her sister's child
back to England and reared it as her own?"

"Er—not quite the end, sir," said Savage. "Sir
Libertine is a merciless animal." He heard Furness's
sharp intake of breath and smiled. "Perhaps he
feared that poor Rose would make the true facts of
his treachery known, which would surely spell his
ruin. Suffice it to say that he embarked on a vicious
campaign of slander to discredit her, blackening her
reputation to such effect that on the one occasion she
dared to appear in public, she was treated so cruelly
that she was heartbroken. In fact, with a disgraceful
lapse of chivalry, the gentleman who had persuaded
her to attend this—er, occasion, and who should by
rights have championed her, himself turned his back
when rumour whispered, and left a more generous
friend to escort her home."

Suspicions were thoroughly aroused now. Furness's name was whispered about, several gentlemen

were on their feet, all scowling at the baronet, and it was clear that feelings ran high. Sir Conrad began to edge away, only to find an immovable Peter Cliveden on one side of him, and an equally immovable Sir Everard Paynton on the other.

"However, I will conclude my tale on a happier note, gentlemen," said Savage, raising his voice above the hubbub. "Sir Libertine was so moved by the lady's plight at the ball that he relented. He has relinquished all claim to the child, purchased a charming villa outside Rome, and registered it in Rose's name. Ample funds have been placed at her disposal, and she and the child will live in comfort and security for the balance of their lives."

"I should jolly well think so!" exclaimed Major Tobbington.

"It don't excuse his black-hearted brutality," argued the admiral.

"Just so," shouted Blainville. "Because of his villainy a fine gentleman died before his time, and his beautiful daughter was as good as murdered!"

"Moreover, her gallant sister was made into an outcast," growled Lord Swann. "It is conduct that would be unforgivable in a simple working man, much less in a gentleman of Quality who has been bred up in the Code of Honour! The rogue should be brought to book, damme!"

Savage laughed softly. "Well, gentlemen, what do you say to my fairytale?"

For a moment they looked disconcerted.

His head slightly lowered, his shoulders hunching forward, Furness watched Savage with a fixed murderous glare.

Then, an embarrassed laugh went up.

Wansford said, "Jove, if you didn't properly ensnare us all in your shocking story of betrayal, Leo. Own up, now. The entire thing was a lie—yes?"

"And jolly well done," said the admiral, who loved a good tale.

"As a matter of fact," drawled Leopold. "...No."

A dead silence.

Furness jolted, his hands clenching and unclenching, that lethal glare still fixed on Savage.

"I am sorry to say that it was all quite true," said Leopold clearly. "My conclusion—only—was an outright lie."

Appalled, Lord Blainville gasped, "*True?* By God—I can scarce credit that such a soulless bounder should walk the earth! A slug has more decency!"

Savage shrugged. "If you doubt me, gentlemen, ask Furness there. He can vouch for the truth of what I've said."

The crowd converged on the baronet, and the growls and mutterings of rage grew louder.

Facing ruin and disgrace, Furness put on a bold front. "Damned if I know what the silly fella's talking about," he shouted. "I've nothing to do with the matter, I promise you."

As all eyes turned back to him, Savage essayed a sweeping bow. "Gentlemen—I go down to defeat. In my wildest dreams I could not top the lie Conrad Furness has just uttered!"

It was the last straw. With a sound somewhere between a howl and a snarl, the maddened Furness eluded Paynton's belated clutch for him, and sprang foward. He struck so fast and so hard that Leopold was hurled back and went down hard.

Dazed, he propped himself on one elbow and gasped, "You'll second me . . . Pay?"

"If he won't, sir," roared Lord Swann furiously, "any gentleman in this room will count it an honour!"

Shouts for tar and feathers arose. Trapped in a storm of contempt and disgust, Sir Conrad Furness, hurling wild threats and imprecations, had to fight his way from the room he was never to enter again.

Mr. Boswell Savage bent over his son and dabbed a handkerchief at his cut mouth. "So *that* is what you were up to, you rascal," he said.

Leopold grinned at him. "That's it, sir."

CHAPTER NINE

THE MORNING WAS COLD and damp, fog drifting wraithlike over the wet grass and only occasionally revealing the two elm trees that gave the famed duelling ground its name.

The distance having been paced off, the darkly clad protagonists took their places, the long and deadly pistols held down at their sides.

"Damned fog," muttered Paynton worriedly.

"It may lend an element of chance," said Cliveden. "Otherwise, they're so blasted well-matched..." He glanced at his companion and didn't finish the sentence.

Paynton shook his head. "I wish to God they fought with swords. Pistols are so curst deadly."

"Don't think it would make a jot of difference in this case, Pay. Furness has nothing to lose. Only look at the fellow."

On this fateful morning, Sir Conrad presented a very different appearance from the suavely distinguished Bond Street beau London knew. His hair was dishevelled, his movements jerky and erratic as though he could scarcely command his emotions, his eyes darted about wildly, and his handsome features were distorted by an almost insane malevolence.

Sir Everard said gravely, "Aye. He looks properly ready for Bedlam. I fancy he considers this to be a killing matter."

Furness most decidedly considered this to be a killing matter, and watching his adversary across the level strip of grass, he said harshly, "A fine return you give me for my friendship, Savage."

"A deal more than you deserved, I agree." Savage's calm self-possession seemed to further infuriate the other man as he went on, "I'd heard rumours, of course, but wouldn't believe 'em. Should have known my father was right, though. He warned me you were a bad man."

The pistol in Furness's hand lifted slightly.

Cliveden shouted, "Hey!"

Paynton started forward, his own pistol raised.

Furness's hand was lowered again. Through his teeth, his voice shaking with passion, he snarled, "You damned traitor. You're about to learn exactly how bad I can be, Savage!"

Mr. Chetley, one of Furness's seconds, was calling the count, his nervous tenor voice slicing through the sudden hush.

"One . . . Two . . . *Three!*"

The final word was half drowned by the two shots that cracked deafeningly but not quite simultaneously.

Smoke and fog billowed.

With an exclamation of dismay, Cliveden began to run.

Beside him, Paynton groaned. "Good thing we brought two surgeons...!"

IT WOULD HAVE TO GO, of course, thought Primrose Hythe, frowning at the irregular henhouse. It would be difficult, because Consuela loved it so. But—go it must. Each time she came outside, she saw it. And every time she saw it, she thought of the sadistic Savage. The very conjuring of his name brought rage seething up. Infuriatingly, as always, hurt and bewilderment followed. It was so incomprehensible that the same man who had abandoned his haughty elegance to chop wood, wash a reluctant cat, and tend three sick people; the same man who had been so tender to a sad child, could have blackmailed her into helping him mortify his family. And not content with subjecting her to such nightmarish humiliation had, with true infamy, then turned his back on her without a second thought.

It was quite windy this afternoon, and a gust sent her pretty new apron billowing out. Her instinctive snatch at it was unfortunate. The blue gingham frill had caught on a nail which, having been hammered in at an angle, protruded slightly. Primrose's tug resulted in a large tear. "Oh! You—*accursed* thing!" she wailed, and kicked the offending henhouse, which accomplished nothing more helpful than to hurt her toes.

With cruel perversity, her treacherous mind summoned up Leo's face, his mouth unsmilingly severe even as the blue eyes sparkled with laughter... She felt his strong arms sweeping her up, holding her close... Heard the lazy drawling voice, "Desist, Spotted Hythe!"

To dwell on those precious moments was utter folly, for it only invited heartbreak. She had to concentrate instead on the way he had treated her at the ball... when he had looked so handsome in his evening dress, his dark curls so charmingly— 'Idiot!' she thought stormily. His eyes were what she must remember—full of that icy hauteur, looking down at her as if she were something considerably less appetizing than a wart on—

"Brettoe's bringed someone to see us, Mama," said Consuela.

Primrose spun round, her heart thundering. But the tall, cadaverously thin gentleman talking agitatedly to Cousin Barrett, was the Reverend Mr. Underhill. It was as well, she thought, because if Leopold Savage ever dared show his horrid face here, she would hope to have at least a rolling pin—preferably a claymore—within easy reach!

Concealing these sinful desires, she smiled and put out her hand. "Good afternoon, Vicar. Consuela, run and ask Aunt Netty to put the kettle on."

Mr. Underhill patted the child on the head and watched her skip away, singing to herself. Turning to Primrose, his lined countenance was even more doleful than usual. "My dear—I have done a terrible thing. A very naughty thing, God forgive me! But—perhaps I was justified. For I fear they were— And in view of all the gossip, I thought— So, I sent them in the wrong direction, do you see?"

She had seldom seen so murderous an expression on Barrett's usually mild face, and it was clear that poor Mr. Underhill was greatly upset. With a miserable premonition of disaster, she said, "I'm afraid I do not understand, sir. What gossip? And whom did you send away?"

"That filthy swine—" began Elstow, furiously.

Mr. Underhill shuddered, and threw up one hand. "Pray control yourself, my boy. It is bad, I agree, but— The case is, Mrs. Primrose, that I chanced to be returning from Portsmouth this morning, and popped into The Merry Monk to have a cup of tea, for it was a blustery drive and I felt quite chilled. At the next table was a party of ladies and gentlemen from London. They spoke quite loudly. I could not help but overhear. And—well, dear lady, I scarce know how to tell you, but—"

Elstow interrupted harshly, "It's that damned Savage. He evidently had a famous time, spreading the details of your personal history all over his club! London rings with it! As if the bastard hadn't brought you sufficient grief!"

"Barret!" cried the Vicar, scandalized. "Moderate your language, I beg!"

Primrose was suddenly icy cold. She had thought she'd known the depths of disillusion, but now came this new grief, striking like a knife at her foolish heart. Anguished, she whispered, "But—he gave me his word...!"

"Did he!" exclaimed Elstow. "Well, that turns the trick, by God!" He went stalking back to the house.

"Oh, dear, oh dear!" moaned the gentle Mr. Underhill, wringing his hands. "Perhaps I should not have come. But I thought— In view of—er, everything... And I am very sure they were Londoners, dear ma'am. I feared they might even be writers for the newspapers, for this is just the kind of sensational tale they dote on."

Fighting to be sensible, Primrose said, "Forgive me, but I cannot quite grasp this. Do you say some gentlemen from London were asking for me?"

"Why, yes, dear ma'am. Whatever did you think I'd been telling you? Their carriage drove up as I left

the inn, and I assured them I did indeed know where
the Widow Hythe lived. But then I remembered what
I had just heard, and I thought, if it is all truth, the
poor little lady has been treated most evilly, and will
want some time to collect herself. So I sent them on
the road to More-or-Less. It was very wicked, but
you are one of my flock, and if you stand in need of
protection, it is up to me to do whatsoever I may,
even to the extent of uttering an outright false-
hood!''

Somehow, she was thanking him for his kindness,
assuring him that she was not going to faint, but was
perfectly all right, hearing his stammered excuses for
not staying to take tea, and watching him hurry off
as if he could scarce wait to shake the dust of Erskine Abbey from his boots.

She could not face Barrett and Netty. Not for a
minute or two. She turned her back to the house, and
struggled to compose herself. Leopold Savage's infamy knew no bounds, it would seem. Not content
with publicly shaming her, he had sunk to the lowest
act a gentleman could commit—he had broken his
given word. He was as dishonourable as he was
heartless...

She found that she was clinging to the wretched
henhouse, and stared at her hand numbly. Furness
would come for Consuela now. Perhaps—oh, God
forbid!—perhaps his was the carriage Mr. Underhill

had sent in the wrong direction. Panic began to rule her. She must act quickly. Consuela must be taken away—somewhere! Anywhere!

She swung round, picked up her skirts, prepared to run to the house, and stopped dead.

Leopold Savage, his high crowned beaver set at its habitually jaunty angle on his head, an amber cane in one hand, was coming towards her, as elegant, as poised, as if he were guilty of none of the evil he had wrought.

Her hands crooked into claws. "Snake!" she hissed between her teeth. "Treacherous—monster!"

Mr. Savage checked. "Eh?"

Before she could hurl herself at him and scratch his deceitful face, Elstow had sprinted up and wrenched him around. The amber cane fell and Savage staggered. "You *damnable,* unmitigated—" snarled Elstow, his arm flying up.

In a instant of terror Primrose knew that if Barrett challenged this dangerous man to a duel, she would lose him, and she could bear no more sadness. Galvanized to action, she sprang between them and seized her beloved cousin's upraised fist. "No! Barrett, you must not!"

Staring past her, his eyes wide, Elstow said, "But—I didn't even touch him!"

Primrose jerked round. Savage was sprawled at her feet, propped on one elbow. His hat had fallen, and she saw now that he was very haggard, and that despite a flickering grin, his eyes were full of pain.

The past was as if wiped away, and she was on her knees beside him. "What is it? Are you ill?"

"Carpenter...pox," he panted. "Lend a hand, will you, old boy?"

"No," said Elstow, scowling but puzzled. "After what you did to Prim?"

Savage sighed, and his head sagged.

The widow threw her arms about him. She heard him gasp, and felt him flinch away. "You're hurt!" she exclaimed, tearing his driving coat open.

"At it...again," he said feebly. "D'ye see, Barrett? Can't keep her hands off me."

He wore neither coat nor waistcoat, and Primrose stared at a shirt with the left sleeve cut away. Her fingers rested very gently upon the bulk of bandages. Searching his pale face, she demanded, "What have you been up to?"

"He's hurt his shoulder!" exclaimed Elstow, peering excitedly. "I'll wager he's been out with someone!"

"Who?" demanded Primrose, her heart beginning to gallop at an extraordinary rate.

The picture of maligned innocence, Savage blinked at her.

Sir Everard Paynton came up at the run. "You blasted idiot!" he said breathlessly, "I *said* you were not fit to go!"

"No choice, Pay." Savage gave a wan smile. "And despite my pitiable state, only see how I am treated! Help me up, will you?"

"No!" said Primrose, drawing him a little closer.

He settled his dark head on a very pleasant pillow, and changed his mind. "On second thought, dear boy, just—go away."

"Before you do," said Primrose. "Tell me. What has he done?"

"Used your history for his tale at the Liars' Club," said Paynton.

"Hoped it wouldn't come to that, m'dear," put in Savage contritely. "I offered him a way out, first, but the silly fellow wouldn't take it."

Paynton nodded. "That's true. Jolly dangerous with a scoundrel like Furness, but Leo thought he owed it to him. Fancies himself a rattlesnake." He saw their incredulous glances and elaborated hurriedly, "Feels obliged to give a man warning, fair and square. He called on Furness the day before the Liars' Club Match, and confronted him with his crimes, and told him to make amends, or the facts would be in all the newspapers. Furness laughed, and boasted that he had done nothing worse than marry a foolish woman who had died. Leo told him flat out that he was a blackguard and had been directly responsible for the deaths of two innocent people.''

"My heavens," gasped Primrose. "Sir Conrad is not the man to take that!''

"Very true, ma'am. He was enraged, but I suspect he wanted no public outcry on such a matter. He warned Leo that even were it all true, there was not a thing anyone could do about it, and that if Leo stirred up any kind of scandal he would pay dearly for his interference. All London knows how deadly Furness is with the pistols, and I suppose he thought Leo would never dare provoke him to a duel. I'll tell you frankly, Mrs. Primrose, when Leo started to tell your poor sister's story at the club, I thought Furness would have an apoplexy. I hope I never again see such an expression on a man's face!''

Elstow's eyes lit up. "Hurrah! Justice at last! How I'd love to have been there! So they fought, did they, sir?''

Reading Savage's gaze correctly, Paynton nodded and, leading the young man away, said, "Indeed they did. Furness was fairly slathering with rage, y'see. Knocked Leo down, so there wasn't nothing to be done, but..." His voice faded.

Savage appeared to have gone to sleep. Primrose touched his cheek very gently. "Tell me one thing, Leopold Byrne Savage. Why did you force me to go through that terrible evening?''

He opened his eyes. "My poor little love. But it was very necessary, you see. I had to put you into a situation that must win their remorse and sympathy when the facts were made known. The—" he caught his breath for a second "—the more cruelly you were treated, the more bravely you behaved, the more they would later realize that you are truly a lady of Quality, and discount what Furness had said of you. You did magnificently, dearest girl, and there is no question but that you will now be received by the ton with open arms. They can be very kind when their hearts are touched."

"So you fought that evil man," she said softly. "And got yourself shot, and are now lying here, pretending you are not ill and in pain, all for my sake."

His lips quirked. "I also lust after the blue scarf," he admitted.

"It is all finished and ready for you, my very dear." Smiling lovingly, she bent to kiss him.

He was not, evidently, too weak to return her embrace, and she was decidedly breathless when she drew back. "You must to your bed before you run a fever," she said. "I am so grateful that you came to tell me, but now I shall have to leave you. He will come after Consuela, and I will not allow her to be treated as he treated my beloved sister."

"We will both leave, just as soon—"

"No, no. You are in no condition for a desperate flight. And besides, you must not leave your home, your family, only for my sake!"

"Oh. Well, how would it be if I left them—for *my* sake?"

"For—*your* sake? Why—"

"The thing is that The League of Henhouse Builders became so incensed when they learned of my new design, that hired assassins are even now upon my trail, and if I am to escape, I—"

She put her fingers over his lips, cutting off the light words and, her suspicions now thoroughly aroused, demanded, "Have done with your funning, and tell me this, Mr. Savage—how is Conrad Furness?"

"Deuce take it," he cried resentfully. "Am I to be chastised again? I promise you, Unspotted Hythe, it was not my fault. The wretched fellow was so enraged that he fired before I'd a chance to properly aim. Threw me off a trifle when I was hit. But I actually hadn't decided—not precisely, you know—to put a period to him."

"Oh, good…heavens! You didn't— He isn't…?"

"Er—'fraid he is. A little bit."

"Then—he won't be coming after Consuela? *Ever?*"

"No. Poor chap. But—he really was a very dirty dish, Prim. I'd suspected it for some while, and Lord knows, I'd heard enough. But not until you told me your story did I realize I had turned a deaf ear to far too much. Well, enough of that. And sweet as my pillow is, beloved, the ground's a bit less than comfortable. If I might be given a hand up—''

She tightened her arms. ''Then—you have ruined yourself. You *really* must leave the country!''

''Rather soon, I'm afraid. I fancy the Runners are after me.''

She released him at once and, standing, handed him his cane. He was considerably more spent than he pretended, but with her help he was up at last, and leaning weakly against the henhouse.

''Oh, gracious!'' exclaimed Primrose in belated recollection. ''Your Runners may be very close by! Not an hour since, Father Underhill deliberately misdirected their carriage to More-or-Less!''

''Dashed cooperative of the old boy. You're sure it was the Runners?''

''He said they were gentlemen from London, and they enquired as to where I lived.''

''Aha! Then I rather suspect, m'dear, that it was my father's coachman the Reverend Mr. Underhill flummoxed. Just as well. Grandmama would have been most shocked to see young Elstow knock down a wounded man.''

"Your—Papa...? Your Grandmama...? Coming here...? Oh, you wretch! Barrett didn't even—"

He staggered, and when she leapt to steady him, promptly kissed her forehead. "I simply cannot bear it when you are baffled," he said by way of apology. "Your little face looks so delicious. I fancy you'd have liked Father Underhill to do the thing, my love. But Grandmama is determined her own chaplain must officiate. Such a cantankerous old lady. It's a pity I love her so much. She admires you tremendously, by the way. Papa has brought a Special License, for I don't propose to wander France searching for a Protestant divine to wed us. Should we have the ceremony out here, by my superb edifice, do you think?"

"Superb...!" she echoed, blinking away happy tears.

"I grant you, it leans a trifle," he acknowledged with a sigh. "I have been studying the principles of henhouse architecture, and mean to set the matter to rights. In six months or so, when it is safe for us to come back, you understand. But I've left strict instructions with Grandmama's steward that in the meantime he must find us some leaning hens who might be less inclined to sneer at my efforts."

Laughing, she said, "Cast your eyes inside your edifice, Mr. Savage. It has been usurped, and the occupants don't give a button whether it leans."

Savage peered inside the henhouse. Milor' lay in a basket of straw, surrounded by seven hungry kittens. "Good Gad!" he exclaimed, awed. "Then—Milor'—was another masquerader!"

Primrose saw a luxurious coach rolling in through the gates. Supporting her love's rather uncertain steps, she began to guide him down to the house. "Milor' has become Milady, I grant you. What do you mean—'another'?"

"I mean you, of course, wretched widow. You've absolutely no right to be calling yourself Mrs. Hythe. The sooner you're using the name you were born to assume, lovely one . . . the better."

"I presume you mean that I was born to be called Mrs. Leopold Savage."

He checked, leaning on her rather heavily, but smiling down at her. "Would that distress you, ma'am?"

"It would," she declared, and seeing fear dawn in his eyes, she went on quickly, "for I could not marry without love, sir."

"Wouldn't ask you to."

"But—I have not heard aught of the tender emotion, Mr. Savage."

"I'll own I miss the spotted dimple, but—" The bantering note left his voice. He said tenderly, "Oh, Prim, bravest and most beautiful of impostors. I gave you my heart, I think, in that first moment I saw you with those dainty cobwebs in your glorious hair..."

"There he is, Boswell," exclaimed Lady Hamildown, as she was handed down from the coach. "And— Oh! My heavens! This must be Consuela. Come, you adorable child. Come to your Great-Grandmama."

Attempting a wobbly curtsey, Consuela abandoned it. "You not great," she pointed out judicially. "You a little lady."

Lady Hamildown said wistfully, "Won't you have me, then?"

"Oooh, yes please," said Consuela with a little skip. "Will you *really* be her Gran'ma? How sp'endid! Now her has kittys, an' fluffy chickys, an' a new little Gran'ma!" And she danced eagerly into her ladyship's waiting arms.

Leopold, also pleading his case, said, "Will you do me the very great honour of accepting this...this most unworthy fellow for your husband?"

Her lips a breath away from his, Primrose murmured, "I may have been a Spotted Hythe, but only think how clever I was to send Consuela in search of our knight in shining armour..."

Blinking rather blurred eyes, and with a small hand tight-clasped in her own, Lady Hamildown straightened, sniffed, and met her son-in-law's amused glance.

Recovering herself, she said tartly, "Only look at that idiotic boy! He can scarce stay on his feet, but he's kissing the Widow Hythe!"

"She doesn't seem to mind," observed Boswell Savage, smiling.

He was perfectly correct.

PENNY JORDAN

Sins and infidelities . . .
Dreams and obsessions . . .
Shattering secrets
unfold in . . .

THE HIDDEN YEARS

SAGE — stunning, sensual and vibrant, she spent a lifetime distancing herself from a past too painful to confront . . . the mother who seemed to hold her at bay, the father who resented her and the heartache of unfulfilled love. To the world, Sage was independent and invulnerable— but it was a mask she cultivated to hide a desperation she herself couldn't quite understand . . . until an unforeseen turn of events drew her into the discovery of the hidden years, finally allowing Sage to open her heart to a passion denied for so long.

The Hidden Years—a compelling novel of truth and passion that will unlock the heart and soul of every woman.

AVAILABLE IN OCTOBER!
Watch for your opportunity to complete your Penny Jordan set.
POWER PLAY and SILVER will also be available in October.

HARLEQUIN®
OFFICIAL SWEEPSTAKES
RULES

NO PURCHASE NECESSARY

1. To enter, complete an Official Entry Form or 3"× 5" index card by hand-printing, in plain block letters, your complete name, address, phone number and age, and mailing it to: Harlequin Fashion A Whole New You Sweepstakes, P.O. Box 9056, Buffalo, NY 14269-9056.

   No responsibility is assumed for lost, late or misdirected mail. Entries must be sent separately with first class postage affixed, and be received no later than December 31, 1991 for eligibility.

2. Winners will be selected by D.L. Blair, Inc., an independent judging organization whose decisions are final, in random drawings to be held on January 30, 1992 in Blair, NE at 10:00 a.m. from among all eligible entries received.

3. The prizes to be awarded and their approximate retail values are as follows: Grand Prize — A brand-new Mercury Sable LS plus a trip for two (2) to Paris, including round-trip air transportation, six (6) nights hotel accommodation, a $1,400 meal/spending money stipend and $2,000 cash toward a new fashion wardrobe (approximate value: $28,000) or $15,000 cash; two (2) Second Prizes — A trip to Paris, including round-trip air transportation, six (6) nights hotel accommodation, a $1,400 meal/spending money stipend and $2,000 cash toward a new fashion wardrobe (approximate value: $11,000) or $5,000 cash; three (3) Third Prizes — $2,000 cash toward a new fashion wardrobe. All prizes are valued in U.S. currency. Travel award air transportation is from the commercial airport nearest winner's home. Travel is subject to space and accommodation availability, and must be completed by June 30, 1993. Sweepstakes offer is open to residents of the U.S. and Canada who are 21 years of age or older as of December 31, 1991, except residents of Puerto Rico, employees and immediate family members of Torstar Corp., its affiliates, subsidiaries, and all agencies, entities and persons connected with the use, marketing, or conduct of this sweepstakes. All federal, state, provincial, municipal and local laws apply. Offer void wherever prohibited by law. Taxes and/or duties, applicable registration and licensing fees, are the sole responsibility of the winners. Any litigation within the province of Quebec respecting the conduct and awarding of a prize may be submitted to the Régie des loteries et courses du Québec. All prizes will be awarded; winners will be notified by mail. No substitution of prizes is permitted.

4. Potential winners must sign and return any required Affidavit of Eligibility/Release of Liability within 30 days of notification. In the event of noncompliance within this time period, the prize may be awarded to an alternate winner. Any prize or prize notification returned as undeliverable may result in the awarding of that prize to an alternate winner. By acceptance of their prize, winners consent to use of their names, photographs or their likenesses for purposes of advertising, trade and promotion on behalf of Torstar Corp. without further compensation. Canadian winners must correctly answer a time-limited arithmetical question in order to be awarded a prize.

5. For a list of winners (available after 3/31/92), send a separate stamped, self-addressed envelope to: Harlequin Fashion A Whole New You Sweepstakes, P.O. Box 4694, Blair, NE 68009.

PREMIUM OFFER TERMS

To receive your gift, complete the Offer Certificate according to directions. Be certain to enclose the required number of "Fashion A Whole New You" proofs of product purchase (which are found on the last page of every specially marked "Fashion A Whole New You" Harlequin or Silhouette romance novel). Requests must be received no later than December 31, 1991. Limit: four (4) gifts per name, family, group, organization or address. Items depicted are for illustrative purposes only and may not be exactly as shown. Please allow 6 to 8 weeks for receipt of order. Offer good while quantities of gifts last. In the event an ordered gift is no longer available, you will receive a free, previously unpublished Harlequin or Silhouette book for every proof of purchase you have submitted with your request, plus a refund of the postage and handling charge you have included. Offer good in the U.S. and Canada only.   HQFW-SWPR

HARLEQUIN® OFFICIAL SWEEPSTAKES ENTRY FORM

4-FWRGS-2

Complete and return this Entry Form immediately – the more entries you submit, the better your chances of winning!

- Entries must be received by **December 31, 1991.**
- A Random draw will take place on **January 30, 1992.**
- No purchase necessary.

Yes, I want to win a FASHION A WHOLE NEW YOU Classic and Romantic prize from Harlequin:

Name _____ Telephone _____ Age _____

Address _____

City _____ State _____ Zip _____

Return Entries to: **Harlequin FASHION A WHOLE NEW YOU,**
P.O. Box 9056, Buffalo, NY 14269-9056   © 1991 Harlequin Enterprises Limited

PREMIUM OFFER

To receive your free gift, send us the required number of proofs-of-purchase from any specially marked FASHION A WHOLE NEW YOU Harlequin or Silhouette Book with the Offer Certificate properly completed, plus a check or money order (do not send cash) to cover postage and handling payable to Harlequin FASHION A WHOLE NEW YOU Offer. We will send you the specified gift.

OFFER CERTIFICATE

Item	A. ROMANTIC COLLECTOR'S DOLL	B. CLASSIC PICTURE FRAME
	(Suggested Retail Price $60.00)	(Suggested Retail Price $25.00)
# of proofs-of-purchase	18	12
Postage and Handling	$3.50	$2.95
Check one	☐	☐

Name _____

Address _____

City _____ State _____ Zip _____

Mail this certificate, designated number of proofs-of-purchase and check or money order for postage and handling to: **Harlequin FASHION A WHOLE NEW YOU Gift Offer,** P.O. Box 9057, Buffalo, NY 14269-9057. Requests must be received by December 31, 1991.

ONE PROOF-OF-PURCHASE

4-FWRGP-2

To collect your fabulous free gift you must include the necessary number of proofs-of-purchase with a properly completed Offer Certificate.

© 1991 Harlequin Enterprises Limited

See previous page for details.